Malibu Carmie

Malibu Carmie

Leah Komaiko

Delacorte Press

Published by
Delacorte Press
an imprint of
Random House Children's Books
a division of Random House, Inc.
New York

Visit us on the Web! www.randomhouse.com/kids
Educators and librarians, for a variety of teaching tools, visit us at
www.randomhouse.com/teachers

Library of Congresss Cataloging-in-Publication Data
Komaiko, Leah.
    Malibu Carmie / Leah Komaiko.
        p. cm.
    Summary: When thirteen-year-old Carmie discovers that her divorced mother, who
suffers from Chronic Fatigue Syndrome, was once a well-known Malibu surfer, she
reevaluates the way she views her mother and herself.
    ISBN 0-385-73172-8 (trade)—ISBN 0-385-90209-3 (glb)
    [1. Surfing—Fiction. 2. Mothers and daughters—Fiction. 3. Self-confidence—
Fiction. 4. Chronic fatigue syndrome—Fiction. 5. Divorce—Fiction. 6. Malibu
(Calif.)—Fiction.] I. Title.

PZ7.K8347Mal 2005
[Fic]—dc22

                                                                            2004018407

The text of this book is set in 12-point Goudy.
Book design by Trish P. Watts
Printed in the United States of America
May 2005
10 9 8 7 6 5 4 3 2 1
BVG

For Dick Dale and Stephanie (Dudette) Lane,
and in loving memory of my awesome mother, Dorothy
—LK

Chapter 1

*　✳　　✳　✳
　✳　✳

STAR OF THE CENTURY
By Carmie Hoffman

SCENE ONE:
Daytime. Outside a forty-room mansion. CARMIE HOFFMAN,
a beautiful blond thirteen-year-old girl with long thin legs,
wearing a lilac miniskirt, walks up to the front door. MAXWELL,
Carmie's personal butler, opens the door. Maxwell has on a
tuxedo.

MAXWELL
Good afternoon, Miss Carmie.

CARMIE
Hello, Maxwell. Do you have my perfect orange smoothie
prepared?

Maxwell hands Carmie the perfect orange smoothie in a big
glass.

MAXWELL

I have also brought you your favorite double-chocolate-
chip-with-walnuts cookie.

CARMIE

Very good, Maxwell. Where's Mother?

MAXWELL

In her study, of course, Miss Carmie. Writing her novel.
She has been in there typing all day. She asked me to tell
you she'll see you at five in the parlor for dinner. She
says she has a surprise for you.

CARMIE

A surprise? Cool! I love surprises!

Carmie Hoffman closed her notebook and looked around
her street with a sigh. Then she dialed 818-555-6865 and
kept walking.

"Behold genius," Carmie said into her cell phone. She
tried to smooth her bushy dark hair away from her ear so
that the phone would have a clear patch for landing. "Can
you hear me now?"

"Yes." Jenny laughed into the phone. Her laugh was big
and deep, so Carmie knew she really meant it. "Are you
going to read to me from your latest movie script?"

"I said, 'Behold genius,'" Carmie repeated as she opened
the door to her house. "My movie is, behold, *Star of the
Century*. But what you are about to see is real genius. Live
entertainment!"

"Oh, *goody!*" Jenny laughed as if she'd never had any entertainment in her life. Carmie liked that nobody could make Jenny laugh as hard as she could. "What is it?"

Carmie walked into the living room. Fluff Bucket, Carmie's fourteen-year-old cat, was on the sofa with her leg straight up like a ballerina. She was one year older than Carmie. Carmie called Fluff Bucket her big sister.

There was the clacking, tap-tap sound of her mother typing at the computer. Her eyes were closed. Her thin, sandy-blond hair was piled up in a sloppy bun. Her skin looked old and a little yellow. A headset covered her ears. Carmie felt a little relieved. At least this time her mother was typing and not just asleep next to Fluff Bucket on the sofa.

On Mondays, Tuesdays and Thursdays, Carmie's mother worked for a doctor's office in Studio City. She had to drive about ten minutes to pick up a stack of tapes and files, take it home, type all the words on the tapes and then take them back. Carmie watched her mother for a few seconds.

"Is your mom home? Can she hear you now?" Jenny asked, laughing.

"I don't know," Carmie said. "Let's test this out. Earth to Elaine." She tried to laugh. "Planet Earth phoning for Elaine Hoffman. If your name is Elaine, press the pound key now."

Carmie's mother's eyes opened slightly. Then they closed again. Carmie watched her mother's long, thin fingers gently hitting each key and thought her mother really should have been a famous piano player. Or a TV host, tapping her fingers on the coffee mug on her desk.

Carmie let her yellow backpack slide off her shoulder and onto the hardwood floor. Fluff Bucket jumped and gave Carmie a cold eye.

"Okay, bye, Mom," Carmie said. "I'm going to Hawaii now."

Carmie's mother kept typing.

"Okay," Carmie said into her cell. "Now here comes the genius you've been waiting for."

"Maybe you shouldn't." Jenny's voice sounded nervous. "Maybe your mom's just really tired again. She can't help it that something's the matter with her. Or she's probably just on one of those big doctor deadlines."

"Or maybe she's just dead." Carmie laughed. She was proud of how funny she was. Then all of a sudden she felt as if she might cry. Why couldn't her mom just be normal like everybody else's mother?

Still holding her cell phone, Carmie went into her bedroom and picked up the old Princess phone on her nightstand. She punched in 818-555-6169. That was the number for the phone right next to the computer.

"One ringy-dingy." Carmie laughed. "Two ringy-dingys." Carmie could hear the phone ringing in the other room. She felt her heart tying in knots.

"I'm hearing three lines," Jenny said. "I don't know if I want to do this again."

"Three ringy-dingys," Carmie said more loudly. "If she answers, Jenny, this time I'm just going to say I'm in Hawaii. It's absolutely *hilarious* when she's like this."

"Don't." Jenny laughed. "Just come over. She can't help it. I'm warning you," she said. "I'm hanging up."

Carmie heard a click and then the dial tone.

4

"Hello?" Her mother picked up the phone next to the computer. Her voice sounded slow and tired. "Elaine Hoffman."

Carmie's heart pounded. She dropped the cell phone onto her bed. She hung up the Princess phone and ran into the living room.

"That was just me, Mommy!" Carmie cried. Then she went to the desk and hugged her mother tightly around the shoulders.

"When did you get home?" Elaine smiled and patted Carmie's hand. "I don't think I even heard you. These tapes I have to transcribe today are so complicated."

Elaine placed the headset carefully on the computer. She rubbed her light brown eyes. They looked a little bit runny in the centers. Carmie didn't know exactly what was the matter with her mother. All she knew was that ever since her mom and dad had gotten divorced three years before, her mom had always been tired. She acted as if she had the flu or something. She would be okay for a few days; then she'd get sad and have a high fever. She went to doctors all the time and they all told her different things to do. They said she was sad and maybe she had chronic fatigue syndrome. All that meant was she couldn't stop being tired. Who couldn't already see that? Now she didn't look well again. Carmie hated that her mother acted this way. She knew she had to make her mother feel better.

"So, Mommy." Carmie laughed. "I just called you to find out what's for dinner."

"Just one minute, sweetie," Elaine said, putting the headset back on. "I have to finish typing this last paragraph."

Carmie went into the kitchen and opened the refrigerator. On the top shelf there were a can filled with vanilla protein powder, a hundred little bottles of vitamins and some milk. Carmie helped herself to a big spoonful of protein powder.

"At least it tastes kind of good," Carmie said, opening a can of cat food for Fluff Bucket. She put the can on the counter. Fluff Bucket jumped up.

"Yours probably tastes better," Carmie said. Then she called into the living room.

"Mommy, want me to order a pizza?" Elaine walked into the room. "I can do it on my cell!"

"Not tonight, honey," Elaine said. "Besides, I don't think that's what your father gave you that cell phone for."

Jenny didn't have her own cell phone yet. In fact, Carmie was one of only three girls who'd just graduated from Van Nuys Middle School and had their own cell phones.

Carmie never liked it when her mother started to talk about her father. Especially when her mother looked as if she didn't feel well. Carmie was afraid it would just make her feel sicker and act more strange.

"Aunt Raleigh is coming for dinner tonight," Elaine said. "And she's bringing her casserole."

"I'm doomed!" Carmie threw up her hands. "Aunt Raleigh always brings something healthy and disgusting. Why must I always be starved to death?"

Elaine laughed softly. "Tofu is supposed to be good for you," she said. "Even the doctors on the tapes say so."

Carmie liked it when she could make her mother laugh, even if she wasn't really joking. When Elaine laughed, she laughed for a long time and her face looked different, more like it did before the divorce.

Carmie loved her aunt Raleigh and her uncle Roy, even though Aunt Raleigh was a vegetarian and would never let any of them eat meat.

"Can I go to Jenny's?" Carmie asked.

"I don't know," Elaine said. "I want you here for dinner. I don't want to be wondering where you are."

"I'll take my cell," Carmie said. "I've got to show Jenny more of my movie script. I've been writing a lot."

"Have you practiced your viola today?"

"I'll be home by six," Carmie said quickly. "I'll practice then. I promise."

Carmie ran into the living room and grabbed her backpack off the floor. School had already been out for half the summer, and the only things she had in there were her movie notebook and pens. That was all she needed.

That and a new life.

Chapter 2

STAR OF THE CENTURY
By Carmie Hoffman

SCENE TWO:
Daytime. Outside Jenny's house. CARMIE, a thirteen-year-old tall blond girl, runs toward Jenny's house. Carmie does not want to be late. She is wearing perfect lilac shorts and a pink halter top. This is a very important day. Because today the important legal papers will all be legal.

CARMIE
(voice-over)
Today, Jenny's parents, Joy and Justin Thompson, and Jenny's brother, James, will adopt me and my big sister, Fluff Bucket Hoffman-Thompson. Now nothing can ever go wrong again.

Carmie looked at her pants pocket as she ran down the sidewalk, making sure that her silver cell phone was peeking out just enough for everyone to see it. Today, unfortunately, nobody was in sight.

Carmie slid the phone out and punched in Jenny's number like lightning: 818-555-6865.

One ringy-dingy. Two ringy-dingys.

It was unlike Jenny not to be in her room, especially when she knew Carmie was going to call.

"I've escaped!" Carmie said with a laugh when the answering machine answered.

Jenny picked up the phone, panting. "Quick! Haul buns. Oh my God. You've got to hurry up and get over here. It's happening again!" Then she hung up.

Carmie didn't know what Jenny was talking about, but her heart started to pound. She had to hurry. That was fine with her anyway. The faster she got off her street the better. She ran past the Rodriguezes' house with the swing set in front, and Bill and Ella's house with their red cars in the driveway, sitting up so high off the tires that the cars always looked as if they were on stilts. Only three more houses and Carmie was off Apricot Street and on Matilija. Matilija was about the same as Apricot, and not terribly embarrassing, but it wasn't Hamlin Street. Carmie knew that as soon as she got three more blocks down and turned onto Jenny's street, she would feel better. Hamlin was the rich street, where Carmie knew she belonged.

The sun was beating down its hardest, as it always did in the Valley just before dinnertime. Carmie's legs felt hot in her jeans, rubbing together like water balloons. She ran as fast as she could and then made a left past Van Nuys High

School, where she would be going in just five weeks. Then she turned onto Hamlin.

Carmie ran faster. The street was wide, with big front lawns, like people had in Beverly Hills. In fact, the street was so wide that two times a year the TV show *The B.H.* came to the house next door to Jenny's to tape its exterior shots. Jenny's mom said they did this because Hamlin Street looked like Beverly Hills, where the show took place, but it didn't cost the company as much money to shoot there. Carmie ran past the house with the big stone gates and the giant windows. She passed the house with the life-sized Raggedy Ann doll that sat in the window. Carmie felt happy, pretending she was running to her house. Past the house with the three fancy black cars in the driveway and the house with the two fake lions in front with their mouths open, looking ferocious. Then there were two regular, crummy houses in a row to remind Carmie that this wasn't really Beverly Hills. Jenny's mom said that long ago Hamlin had been one of the most glamorous streets in Los Angeles. The mother of an old dead actor named Clark Gable had lived there, and so had someone famous named Marilyn Monroe. Carmie liked how Jenny's mother knew things like that about Hollywood. Carmie didn't think her own mother even knew how to drive to Hollywood.

Jenny's mother, Joy, had one long, dark blond braid down her back that looked like Jenny's. Jenny's father, Justin, still lived at home with them. Carmie thought they were happy because Justin and Joy sold houses together. Although Carmie had only been ten when her father had moved to Indiana, and her mother never said much about it, she thought for certain he must have left because her mother had been too boring and Carmie had still been too young to do much of anything with.

Carmie picked up speed. Jenny's house was almost the last one on Hamlin. As Carmie got closer, she saw some commotion toward the end of the street. It looked as if policemen on motorcycles were sitting right in front of Jenny's house. Carmie reached for her cell phone. Then, instead of dialing, she just ran.

When Carmie got closer, she saw that the street was lined with cars and big trucks. She looked around for Jenny and her family. Then she saw something that made her heart pound. A man was sitting high up on a chair.

"Quiet. Quiet, people, please," he called out to the crowd. "Lights . . . camera . . . *The B.H.*, scene two, take four. We've got speed."

Chapter 3

Jenny saw Carmie from the front of the crowd. "Is this beyond cool?" she whispered, pulling Carmie close to the front so she could get a good look. The television crew always let the neighbors watch as long as they didn't walk onto the set or make noise.

"Oh my God, yes!" Carmie beamed as she studied all the big studio trucks and the cameras that looked like drums on high stands. She watched Jenny and her mother stand side by side with their perfect matching braids. They could have been a mother-and-daughter team in a movie.

"Hi, darling." Joy squeezed Carmie's hand. "Who knows?" she whispered. "Maybe one day a big studio will be making one of your movies, Carmie."

"That's for sure," Justin said, finding his way over. He was tall, and handsome for an older man.

"Maybe." Carmie blushed. "At your house. Your house is as good as this one."

"Oh no, darling," Joy whispered, and smiled. "I know

this house. This house has an agent. Like a movie star. Our house will never be famous enough to be a movie star." She raised her eyebrows so Carmie could see how silly she thought the whole thing was.

"Quiet on the set!" the director called. "And action!"

"Oh, wow." Carmie giggled softly to Jenny. "Look! Isn't that Katy Lee?"

A gorgeous girl with curly blond hair and blue eyes like a cat's walked out of the house. The camera followed her. Then a microphone dropped to her mouth.

"I can't stop thinking about that blond guy we met today at Johnny Missile's!"

"I bet he can't stop thinking about you, either," another girl said to Katy, following her down the front walk. "He was a real hottie!"

Carmie stared. This was Kiya Rose, the star, with long straight brown hair and the best smile. She looked shorter in real life than on TV. She was probably a few years older than her character, too. Maybe even eighteen. She was perfect. Carmie tried to smooth her hair straight with her fingers.

"Which one do you think is prettier?" Carmie whispered.

"Where's the 'real hottie'?" Jenny whispered back, looking around.

Just then the cameras swung to face a roped-off area in front of the house. A silver Mustang convertible drove up fast to the curb.

"That's got to be either Dan or David," Jenny whispered excitedly. Dan and David were the two big hotties of *The*

B.H. All the teen magazines had posters of them and articles on them every month.

"Zoom in," the director called. "This is a zoom shot, people."

The camera stands rushed forward to the curb. The car door opened. Carmie's heart jumped. It wasn't Dan or David.

The boy who got out of the car had the most perfect sun white-blond hair Carmie had ever seen off television. His skin was completely tan. Carmie thought that was probably from makeup. When he smiled, dimples appeared in his cheeks.

"Who's that?" Carmie whispered to Jenny. "He must be a special guest star."

"That's my new husband," Jenny said. She squiggled her way a little nearer to the front of the crowd and put her hand on her hip.

The beautiful boy lifted what Carmie could now see was a surfboard from the backseat. She had never seen a surfboard up that close in person. He held it firmly under his arm and walked up the sidewalk to the house with the bright lights all over.

"I thought I'd find you girls here," the boy said to Katy and Kiya. "You dropped a piece of paper with your address in the front seat of my car."

"I did, Scott?" Katy tried to smile as if she didn't know what he was talking about.

She sounded so fake that Carmie wanted to laugh. But she couldn't without Jenny there.

"I guess you really wanted to see me again. I never

thought surfers came east of the Pacific Coast Highway," Kiya Rose teased.

"Dude." Scott smiled. "Who doesn't want to come to Beverly Hills?"

"*Cut!*" the director called. "Dude?" He groaned and pulled his baseball cap as far as he could over his eyes. "Okay, where's a writer? Who writes these things? We need a little redo here. Girls, you were fine. Let's take ten, people."

The lights shut off. Carmie watched Katy and Kiya walk to their trailers on the street. She knew that was where they waited between the scenes. Guys in blue jeans with walkie-talkies were everywhere. Carmie's heart beat quickly. This was the second time she had seen the TV crew on Jenny's street. It was also the most exciting thing that had happened all summer. Carmie tried to tell which person was the writer, but there were so many people walking around with pads of paper and boards that she couldn't. She looked around for Jenny, who was walking toward the set, where regular people weren't allowed.

Carmie took out her cell phone as if she was making an important call. Then she sat on the curb, opened her backpack and took out her notebook and pen.

STAR OF THE CENTURY
By Carmie Hoffman

Daytime. Beverly Hills. KATY LEE and KIYA ROSE come out of their house. Their best friend, CARMIE, drives up. She is in a brand-new yellow Hummer.

15

Do you want to go for a picnic at the beach? It would be so perfect to go in your car.

Sure. No problem. I'll drive.

Carmie looked up, and Jenny was walking right toward her with the beautiful boy. She was giggling, and her face looked flushed and ridiculous. The closer they got, the better Carmie could see Scott's face. He really wasn't wearing any makeup.

"Carmie, this is Jon," Jenny said proudly. She opened her eyes wide so only Carmie could see.

"No, I'm Scott," Jon said, teasing her.

"Shut up," Jenny said, laughing, and pretended to poke him. She beamed.

"Hey," Jon said to Carmie.

"Hey," Carmie said. She didn't want to have to get up off the curb, where he could see all of her. She knew she had to lose at least ten pounds.

"Carmie's going to be a screenwriter," Jenny said.

"Oh yeah?" Jon looked down into Carmie's eyes. "That's cool. It's probably better than being an actor."

"You don't like being famous?" Carmie couldn't believe how fast these stupid words flew out of her mouth. She hoped she didn't sound like an idiot.

"It's okay," Jon said, laughing. "But I'm not really famous. I've just done a peanut butter commercial and now

I'm on this show as a guest star. My mom wanted me to do this. She's a big art director for the movies."

"Wow," Carmie said. "I don't think my mother even goes to the movies."

Jon laughed. Carmie stood up. She was now close enough to him to touch his dimples. She liked that Jon could tell she was funny. "You're pretending to be a surfer?" Carmie asked.

"No, I *am* a surfer." Jon smiled at her, so she could see he was for real. "I'm pretending to be an actor who likes Beverly Hills. I'd tank if I lived in Beverly Hills."

Carmie was too startled by what she was hearing to say anything.

"He's a real surfer dude." Jenny laughed, delighted.

"Correct." Jon laughed. "I live at the beach."

"Well, I live next door to here," Jenny said.

"Dude." Jon winked at her. "How do you stand it? You'll fry out here in the Val. Besides"—he looked at Jenny's body—"I'll bet you look real nice in a bikini."

Carmie cringed. She knew he could never say that to her. She told herself not to worry. They weren't going anywhere. Jon didn't know yet that they couldn't drive.

"Which beach?" Jenny smiled. "Santa Monica?"

"No," Jon said, pretending to gag as if he was swallowing something disgusting. "Malibu. The Bu. The only beach. I'm out there every day. You should come. I want to see you again." He took Jenny's hand and squeezed it. "I'll put you on a little Boogie board."

"A Boogie board." Jenny laughed.

17

"Yeah, you know," Jon said. "Like a surf stroller."

"*Okay, let's roll!*" the director called into his megaphone. "Break time is coming to an end, people."

"Now, don't forget me." Jon gave Jenny a little squeeze on her shoulder. Carmie watched Jenny's eyes close. She felt sick.

"You come too, Carmie," Jon said as if he meant it.

Then Carmie and Jenny watched him walk back onto the set. The loud switches of the lights flicked on again.

"Oh my God," Jenny said. "I'm about to faint. We're going. Don't you want to go to the beach tomorrow? We haven't been to the beach once this summer. We can't just swim at the park pool until I have to go to Colorado. Doesn't this sound like the most fun?"

"Oh yeah." Carmie felt like she'd just swallowed something awful. She got up off the curb. She saw a line of people at one of the parked trucks. They were holding plates and cloth napkins, getting their dinner off the truck. The aroma of steak was carrying even in the flat heat. It smelled delicious.

Suddenly Carmie remembered something really awful. Tofu.

"Oh my God, Jenny," she said, checking the time on her cell phone. "I've got to go!"

Chapter 4

BIG STAR OF THE CENTURY
By Carmie Hoffman

NEXT SCENE:

Daytime. The Beach. JON, the gorgeous surfer/actor, CARMIE and JENNY pull into the parking lot in a perfect silver Mustang convertible. Jon is driving. His blond hair glistens in the sun. Carmie is next to him. She is wearing a beige cloth sun hat that matches her new mauve beach cover-up. Carmie puts a little suntan lotion on the tip of her cute nose.

CARMIE

I don't want my nose to look like I put it in the microwave.

Jon laughs. He turns to Carmie and smiles. Then he tugs her cap down over her face a little farther. He is teasing her. Anybody can see he really likes Carmie. Jenny is in the backseat. She laughs at Carmie because Carmie is so funny. It is not a fake laugh.

NO. SCRATCH THAT. I HAVE TO START ALL OVER.

Outside. Malibu Beach. A shiny black limousine pulls into a special cement driving area on the sand. Surfer guys and girls in bikinis run up to the car. Their mouths drop open. Everybody wants to see who is inside. The limo driver, MAXWELL, gets out of the car. He walks around to the door and opens it. A sixteen-year-old beautiful blond girl named CARMIE gets out of the limousine. She is the only person in this big car. She has long, thin, perfect legs and everybody can see them poking out from her new blue and peach cover-up.

MAXWELL

Should I come back for you at four, Miss Carmie?

Carmie reaches into her bag. She pulls out her cell phone. A thousand-dollar bill accidentally falls out of the bag too. Everybody stares.

CARMIE

Yes, Maxwell. That would be fine. Of course, if I want to stay later, I will just call you.

"Can you hear me now?" Carmie said into her cell phone. Jenny laughed. Carmie was walking home from Van Nuys Middle School, holding her viola case in her other hand. The day was hot enough to make her shirt stick to her back. She was going home from Summer Music Workshop. Carmie's mother had signed her up so that she would keep practicing a musical instrument. Summer Music Workshop was for kids all over the Valley, and only the best musicians were allowed in. Carmie liked that she was one of the best. But she didn't like that it was at the viola.

20

"I'm doomed, Jen," Carmie said. "Some kid next to me almost poked me in the eye with his bow today. Now I'm going to sweat to death. My mother doesn't know where I belong. This is the day, I swear. I can't take it anymore. I'll tell my mother I should never go back there."

"This is the day we should be in Malibu," Jenny said as if she was running for president of the United States. "When are we ever going to have this opportunity again? We've never been to Malibu, only Santa Monica. It's so much cooler in Malibu! We can wear our new bathing suits! Plus, when will another actual TV surfer ever invite us to come out there? I don't want Jon to forget me!"

Carmie had been hoping Jenny had forgotten the whole thing.

"What's wrong with just going to the park pool?" Carmie said. Then she paused, afraid Jenny would get mad about her obvious lack of enthusiasm. "Besides, um, did you ask your mom if she'd drive us?"

"Of course," Jenny said. "But that's just the problem. She can't drive us until we come back from our vacation. She and my dad have to sell houses every day. She said she can't get out of it."

Carmie felt herself breathing normally again.

"So can you ask *your* mom?" Jenny asked.

"Today?" Carmie stopped.

"Or, at the worst, tomorrow," Jenny said.

Carmie's mind went blank. She had to figure out fast a way to say no. Her mother would sometimes drive them to the pool because it was close. Most of the time she would drop them off, go grocery shopping and come back. Carmie didn't even mind that her mother sometimes stayed at the pool, because her mother liked to swim so much. She seemed like her old self. When Carmie saw her mother swimming, she felt as if her life was normal. Besides, the pool was just for everybody's parents and sisters and brothers, and there were hardly ever any cute boys.

"My mom?" Carmie laughed. "Are you kidding? Besides, I'm pretty sure she's busy."

"Well, could you just ask her?" Jenny said. "Maybe tomorrow isn't one of the days she works."

"No, it is," Carmie said. "Besides, even the days she doesn't work in the summer, you know how she is—a lot of the time she has to rest so she doesn't get sick."

"She doesn't seem that sick to me," Jenny said. "Besides, summer is almost over. By the time I come back from my cousins' in Colorado, it'll be too late. Why can't you just ask her? What's the worst thing she can say? No?"

* * *

Carmie walked up Apricot Street. She didn't like to lie, but she knew she had to make up a reason her mother couldn't take them. Besides, Jenny would never call Carmie's mother to find out if Carmie was lying. Carmie saw her house and suddenly she felt better. Aunt Raleigh and Uncle Roy's car was in their driveway. Aunt Raleigh always seemed to save the day.

Carmie ran the rest of the way. She opened the door and tried to drop her viola case quietly in the hallway.

"I'm home!" she called out.

"Who is 'I'm'?" Aunt Raleigh said, laughing. Her voice was deep and solid sounding.

"I'm slime!" Carmie laughed.

Aunt Raleigh walked out of the living room. Even though she wasn't much taller than Carmie, her hug was strong.

"Don't you call my niece slime," Aunt Raleigh said, laughing.

"Hi, honey," Carmie's mom called from the sofa. "How was your music practice?"

"It was okay." Carmie rolled her eyes at Aunt Raleigh. "If you don't mind torture."

Aunt Raleigh laughed. Carmie knew that if Aunt Raleigh was her mother, she would be the kind of mother Carmie could ask to drive her places without dying of embarrassment.

"You want torture?" Aunt Raleigh grabbed for Carmie's sides and started tickling. Carmie screamed and tried to pull away. But it was too late.

"No, stop!" Carmie laughed hard. "Please. I beg of you. I'll eat tofu every day for the rest of my life."

Carmie let herself drop to the floor to get away. Fluff Bucket walked between her legs.

"Truce!" Carmie finally squealed, trying to catch her breath. "Truce! It's too hot!"

"You can say that again," Carmie's mother said, walking into the room. "Hi, sweetie." Carmie looked up. Somehow her mother looked good today. As if she was almost happy. "In fact, I was just telling Raleigh this would be a good day to go for a swim. Why don't you call Jenny and ask if she wants to come to the park with us?"

Carmie tried to think fast. "Jenny can't go to the park today," she said. "Her mother won't let her. She was thinking maybe you could take us swimming tomorrow. But I told her tomorrow you have to work."

"No, I don't, honey." Elaine smiled. "As a matter of fact, I'm off the rest of the week."

"Well, let me say hallelujah." Aunt Raleigh laughed.

"Dr. Tash is on vacation and there are no tapes to type. So I don't see why we can't go to the pool tomorrow, too," Carmie's mother said.

Carmie panicked. She had to come up with a lie fast. "But Jenny doesn't want to go to the pool," Carmie heard herself blurt, as if she wasn't even the one talking. "I was wondering, for a change, can you drive us to the beach?"

"Where?" Elaine's smile disappeared. "Santa Monica?"

"No," Carmie said. "Malibu Beach."

Aunt Raleigh looked at Carmie's mom as if she knew something special about Malibu. Carmie's mom gave Aunt Raleigh a look that said, "Don't look at me."

"You can come too, Aunt Raleigh," Carmie said excitedly. "You know how to get there, right?"

"Sure." Aunt Raleigh smiled. "But you know I'm not much of an out-in-the-sun-all-day kind of gal. I'm afraid my beach days are over."

"But you could stay under an umbrella," Carmie said.

Aunt Raleigh looked at her sister. "What do you think, Elaine? Would tomorrow be a good day for you to take Carmie to Malibu?"

"Why Malibu?" Carmie's mother asked. "It's so far. What's the matter with Santa Monica?"

"That's okay, Mommy," Carmie said, relieved. She held her mother's hand. "We don't have to go. Besides, I don't want to get lost."

"Oh, I bet I could still find it," Carmie's mother said, looking at Aunt Raleigh, who smiled.

Carmie watched her mother and her aunt. Something was going on, but Carmie didn't know what it was.

"I haven't been to Malibu in a hundred years," Carmie's mother said. "Sure. We can go tomorrow. But we should leave pretty early."

"But are you sure you're going to want to be there all day?" Carmie asked. "I mean, I don't think there're any waiting areas there for parents."

"Are you kidding?" Aunt Raleigh gave a big laugh. "Your mother belongs at Malibu. Don't you know? Do you have any idea who your mother is?"

"Yes," Carmie said, kissing her mother and her aunt. "Very funny, you guys." Then she ran down the block to go tell Jenny the news.

"I know who my mother is," Carmie said to herself. "She's a loser."

Chapter 5

BIG STAR OF THE CENTURY
By Carmie Hoffman

Nighttime. Van Nuys, California. Everything is fine until all of a sudden an earthquake shakes the Hoffman residence. A window smashes. The electricity shuts off. CARMIE finds a flashlight and turns on her special radio.

RADIO ANNOUNCER
This was a tumbler. All roads to Malibu are being shut down. I repeat, the Malibu road police have closed down the roads to Malibu until further notice.

There was a knock on Carmie's bedroom door. "You can come in," Carmie said, closing her writing notebook. Carmie's mother walked into the room, carrying a huge stack of laundry. Fluff Bucket was resting on top of the pile.

"Princess Fluff," Carmie said, lifting the cat high into the air.

"Your new bathing suit is in there," Carmie's mother said, putting the clothes on Carmie's bed.

Carmie had worn the new bathing suit only three times. It was a blue two-piece. She really didn't like it as much as her old one, which had bottoms that were more like shorts, but that suit was completely faded.

"Thanks, Mommy," Carmie said. "Are my blue jeans in there too? I'll just wear them over my suit."

"Oh, sweetie," Elaine said. "What's wrong with your cover-up? It will be so much cooler." Elaine lifted a white terry cloth dress from the stack. It was what Carmie always wore to the pool. It had thin straps, big pockets and one big flower. For the first time, it looked to Carmie as if it was for a baby.

"That's okay, Mommy," she said. "It's too worn-out looking."

Suddenly Carmie thought of her mother in the bathing suit that she wore to the pool. Carmie cringed. It was blue and all one piece, and it looked as if it was two hundred years old.

"*You* should get a new bathing suit," Carmie said.

"Why?" Elaine asked. "The one I have is fine." She sat down beside Carmie, pointing at Carmie's notebook. "How is the movie script coming today? Do you want to read to me?"

"No thanks," Carmie said. "I couldn't come up with a story today."

"Well then, how about your viola?" Elaine asked. "I don't hear you practicing."

"I practiced," Carmie said. "Yesterday. Plus I played all day at school."

"Mr. Adler said you could be a very gifted musician if you take this seriously," Elaine said. "I think it is wonderful that you know how to play an instrument. You'll enjoy having that all your life. Besides, maybe you could grow up to be in a professional orchestra like Mr. Adler."

"I want to grow up to be a screenwriter," Carmie said.

"You can always write movies later when you get a little older," Elaine said. "It's harder to learn an instrument as you get older."

"I'll still learn the viola when I'm older," Carmie insisted.

"Well, we'd better get to sleep," Elaine said. Her voice was starting to sound very tired. "Tomorrow's an early day. Time to put away your notebook."

"I don't know how to start it anyway," Carmie said.

"How about 'once upon a time'?" Elaine's voice started to trail.

"Not once upon a time, Mommy." Carmie tried to laugh at how little her mother knew. "Movie stories always start with 'fade in,' not 'once upon a time.' "

*   *   *

Jenny and Carmie helped put the cooler in the backseat of Elaine's old car and got in with it.

"Thank you for driving us, Elaine," Jenny said. She tugged the sun visor on Carmie's head down to her nose.

"Nice." Carmie giggled.

"I hope it's not overcast at the beach," Elaine said. "Especially for your first time at Malibu. We might see some good surf out there."

Carmie smiled. Her mother's voice sounded awake and happy and as if she even knew what she was talking about.

"Wow, Elaine," Jenny said, as if she really meant it. "I bet you know more about the beach than my mom does."

Carmie looked at Jenny. She wasn't even sure her mother knew how to drive to the beach. She tried to remember the last time she'd gone to the beach with her mother. Every summer Jenny's mom or dad took them to Santa Monica. Then, suddenly, Carmie remembered being in the water with her father. She saw herself sitting high up on his shoulders in her bathing suit with the strawberries on it. She was laughing. She saw her father's navy blue plaid swimming trunks. Carmie remembered how funny it felt to hold on to his big shoulders and touch his sopping-wet black hair. She was six. He was laughing.

Jenny and Carmie looked out the window.

"When we get there," Jenny said, "I'm running straight into the water. Well, maybe first I'll take my shorts off." She laughed.

"Aren't you going to look for that Jon guy first?" Carmie asked so her mother couldn't hear.

"No way." Jenny laughed too loudly. "I want to hang out with you. Besides," Jenny said, as if she was a grown-up woman, "don't you remember *The B.H.?* Like in the show, Jon should be looking for me!"

Carmie looked at Jenny's legs beside hers on the seat.

They weren't skinny, but they looked muscular. They were tan enough to make her pink shorts look good. All Jenny had on top was her bikini. She could really be a Beverly Hills girl if she wanted to be. Carmie tried not to look at Jenny's breasts. Everybody knew Jenny had the biggest breasts of all the girls in their class. But Jenny didn't ever seem to act as if they were anything great.

"So, race me to the water?" Jenny slapped Carmie on her blue-jeaned leg.

"I'll probably just stay with my mom at first," Carmie whispered. "Just in case she starts to feel tired again. I don't want her to be nervous."

Carmie watched the back of her mother's head as she drove. Elaine had her favorite station playing—the one with boring people just talking to each other. Carmie tried to laugh quietly with Jenny about how slowly Elaine was driving. She always drove slowly.

"Do you want me to call, Mommy, and find out the real way?" Carmie asked. "I've got my cell." Carmie checked to be sure it was peeking perfectly out the corner of her backpack.

"That's okay," Elaine said. "I think there's a shortcut here."

Elaine turned off the freeway and onto a windy, open canyon road. Carmie had never seen it before.

"We're in a canyon," Jenny said. She rolled down her window a little, looked out and smiled.

"It's beautiful," Carmie said, hoping her mother could stay on the road. Carmie looked out the window as they drove down and down into the canyon until all she could see was the Pacific Ocean.

"It's eighty-two beautiful degrees at Malibu already," an announcer's voice said on the radio. "Water's a decent sixty-eight, much warmer than yesterday. It's pretty small, but we may get some two- to three-foot sets coming in."

The sun was shining brightly. Elaine pulled slowly into a parking lot. It had a sign that said WELCOME TO MALIBU BEACH. It was small, as if it was private, unlike the one at Santa Monica, which everybody in Los Angeles could fit into. And unlike in Santa Monica, everybody here looked perfect.

"You can go a little bit faster, Mommy," Carmie said. "There's a big parking space with no other cars around on the other side."

"Okay, dear," Elaine said softly. She pulled slowly into the space. Then the three of them jumped out of the car and headed for the sand.

Chapter 6

*

    *   *   *

        *   *

"Oh, wow," Jenny said, looking all around. "This is so incredibly cool!"

"Yeoowch!" Carmie jumped as soon as her feet hit the beach.

"Put your thongs on, Carmie," Elaine said. "You'll burn your feet in this sand."

Carmie ran ahead as if she was on hot coals.

"Put on your *thongs*!" Jenny laughed at the old word. "And keep going."

Carmie ran farther onto the beach. She ran past girls with long hair and long legs and the perfect amount of suntan lotion in small white dots on their noses. Just like in the movies, their bathing suits were even smaller than bikinis.

Malibu looked like a gigantic beach blanket just big enough for the people who belonged there.

"Thongs!" Elaine called out again. Carmie kept running.

"How's this?" she called, sitting down on a spare patch of

sand. "Is this cool?" She shouted loudly so that the teen-
agers around her could hear. Carmie felt the hot sand
climbing up her pants. She was the only one on the beach
wearing blue jeans. She reached into her backpack and
pulled out her cell phone.

The sun on the shiny silver of the phone made a shoot-
ing reflection that bounced onto the faces of two girls
sleeping on the next towels. One girl propped herself up
on her elbows. Carmie thought she was probably seven-
teen. Her blond hair was wet and matted on her back. One
eye was closed to block out the reflection. With the other
eye, she gave Carmie a long dirty look. Carmie just hoped
the girl didn't notice she was there with her mother.

"Great," Carmie heard the girl say to her friend. "Lucky
us. We're stuck next to the Val." Then she collapsed back
onto her towel.

Carmie's mother approached. She looked so old, as if she
might just faint in the sand.

"Oh my God." Jenny laughed hard, running up to
Carmie. "This is a million times better than *The B.H.*"

Carmie swallowed hard. The girls on the towels both sat
up and looked.

"Well, well," Elaine said softly, looking around. She
opened her sun umbrella. "It's the same beach," she said.

"Isn't this great?" Jenny asked. She took in a deep breath
of clean ocean air, closed her eyes and smiled at the sky.

"This is a blast," Carmie agreed.

"But where are the boys?" Jenny asked too loudly.

Carmie looked at her mother. She was busy putting suntan lotion on her pasty white legs. Carmie wondered if her

mother could hear the rap music playing on a radio right behind her. Those weren't the kinds of words she wanted to listen to around her mother.

"Look!" Jenny laughed. "There's a whole litter of them out there."

Carmie looked at the ocean and saw a hundred blond heads bobbing in the water. In the middle of them Carmie thought she could spot a few girls, and more on the sides. The stretch of ocean looked hardly bigger than the sand. There weren't any waves. Just surfers packed together like birds perched on long branches waiting for the right moment to fly.

"One of them has to be Jon," Carmie said quietly to Jenny.

"They all look ridiculous." Jenny laughed. "Come with me and get a better look?"

"In a minute," Carmie said. "I'm just going to make sure my mom's okay first."

Jenny looked at Carmie as if the sun had already gone to Carmie's head. "Then, is it okay if I go in, Elaine?" Jenny asked.

"Okay, but you've got to be very careful," Elaine said. "This is a surfing beach and when those waves come in, if you're swimming in the break water, some guy's going to plow right into you with his board. So don't go out very far."

"I won't, Elaine," Jenny promised. Then she quickly took off her shorts. "Come down," she said to Carmie.

Carmie watched the girls on the towels beside her look

34

at Jenny. Then she watched her best friend walk slowly down to a new world. A world that Carmie was afraid of.

"Aren't you hot, honey?" her mother asked.

"Not yet," Carmie said. She rolled up the cuffs of her jeans. She looked at her mother in her old blue bathing suit. For that moment, Carmie was happy to have her mother there by her side.

"Turn around, sweetie, and I'll put some lotion on your back," Carmie's mother said. "Okay?"

"Okay," Carmie said. The lotion and her mother's long fingers felt good on her skin.

"Want some too?" Carmie asked. She smoothed the lotion over all the little brown spots on her mother's back. "Thank you for bringing us here, Mommy," she said.

"Oh, you are so welcome, sweetie." Elaine smiled bigger than Carmie had seen in a long time. "I'm happy to be one of you girls," she said, giggling. "You may not actually believe this, but I used to come here when I was younger."

"Oh." Carmie just smiled.

"Dude." Carmie suddenly heard a boy walking up behind them. He had sandy-brown hair and long surfer trunks. His chest was tan and completely dry.

"I can't believe how totally flat it is."

Carmie looked down nervously at her bathing suit top.

"I hear you, brah," another boy said. He was shorter than the first boy, and Carmie was sure he wasn't any older than she was. "All those guys out there and no surf. I'm bummin'."

"Yeah, well then, let's haul," the first boy said. "Lemme just go get my board."

Just then the older boy got a good look at the girls on the towels.

"Fine," the younger boy said.

"Yowza," the older one said, stopping. Then they kept walking.

Carmie's heart pounded. She knew they weren't saying that about her, but she was relieved that her mother was under her umbrella with her eyes closed. Carmie wiggled her toes in the sand. She felt happy to be in the sun. For the first time in her life, she could say she was at Malibu. She lay down and closed her eyes.

*　　*　　*

"Dude, wake up!" Carmie heard Jenny's loud happy laugh right over her. She opened her eyes. Cold water fell off Jenny onto Carmie's legs. Jenny had three cute surfers with her. Carmie crossed her arms over her chest.

"These are my new friends," Jenny announced, as if she really meant it. Carmie saw that one of the boys was Jon. Up this close, he looked even cuter than when he was in Van Nuys and wearing clothes. The other two guys were blond and more regular-looking, but still cuter than any boy in the Valley.

"Hey," Carmie said.

"Hey," Jon said. The other two boys laughed as if they were in on a private secret.

"And this is my best friend, Carmie," Jenny announced

even more loudly. Then she pointed at Elaine. "That's Carmie's mom. But I think she's asleep."

"Or dead," Carmie said, trying to seem funny.

"Come on, Jenny," Jon said, smiling big so that Carmie could see his dimples. He stuck his surfboard deep into the sand. "I'm waiting for that suntan lotion rub you promised me."

"Oh, shut up." Jenny laughed as if she was talking to her brother. "Let me get dried off first."

Jenny lifted her towel. Flying sand hit the girls on the towels and they both propped themselves on their elbows to get a good look. Carmie could tell the girls thought Jon was cute. The boys watched Jenny dry her legs and then her top.

"You are frosted," Jon said, unable to take his eyes off her.

"You're frosted flakes." Jenny laughed. The girls on the towels looked at each other as if they couldn't believe how lame Jenny was. "You make me laugh, Jon," Jenny said.

Carmie checked whether her mother was still asleep.

"I don't know about you Val ladies," Jon said, putting his arm around Jenny, "but I'm on empty. I need food."

"I'll catch you later, dude," the first boy said. He gave Jenny another look-over. Then he headed to the shore.

"Get me a dog, brah, will you?" the second boy said, sitting down in the sand. "I've got the dead presidents in my car."

"I'll take a dog too, please." Jenny smiled up at Jon so he could see how perfect her teeth were.

"You gonna come with me and get it?" Jon smiled.

"I could," Jenny teased, "but I'd rather watch you walk." She sat down on her towel beside Carmie.

Jon smiled and shook his head. "All right," he said slowly and flirtatiously. "But I'm leaving this board here with you. It's in your protection. And it's not a Boogie board."

"Brah." Jenny laughed. "I'll guard it like a pit bull."

"You won't take it out, will you?" Jon teased.

"Dude," Jenny said. "Don't sweat it. I wouldn't even know how to use one of these things."

The girls on the towels just stared at Jenny. Carmie felt proud to be on the right blanket. As long as the boys went away before her mother saw them.

"Well, if it starts rippin' out there before I get back and you can't help yourself, you can take it."

"Thanks," the sitting boy said.

"Not you, brah." Jon laughed. "You'll do it. Just Jenny." Then he glanced at Carmie and her mother. "And you girls, too," he said, and winked.

Elaine sat up. She looked at the board plunged into the sand close to her.

"That's a surfboard, Mommy," Carmie said confidently.

"It's my new friend Jon's," Jenny said, watching Jon head up to the food truck.

"Oh," Elaine said, looking at the board. It had purple and red racing stripes on it. "Very colorful!"

"He said we could use it," Jenny said with a laugh. She stood up and positioned herself back to back with the board. "This is cool!" Jenny said, a little too loudly. "Carm, our first real live surfboard!"

38

Carmie smiled. She wondered what the boy sitting beside them was thinking about this conversation. He just stared at the ocean.

"Who's taller?" Jenny asked, trying to measure her height against the board.

"You're taller, Jenny." Elaine laughed. "You should have seen the old fiberglass boards. They were so long!" Carmie watched her mother stare at the surfboard. She didn't look right and Carmie was afraid she was getting one of those fevers again. Then Elaine stood up. The boy in the sand stood up too. Carmie saw surfers in the ocean on their stomachs on the boards, paddling farther out.

She looked at her mother. "Don't you want to sit down, Mommy?" she asked.

"There's a set coming in," Elaine said, smiling.

"Is that okay?" Carmie asked.

Elaine just watched. A few guys stood up from their blankets. They had short wet suits on and looked like seals. They tucked their surfboards under their arms and started running to the shore.

Carmie looked out at the ocean. She could see the beginnings of waves coming in like foothills, rising and then falling.

"Surf's up!" Jenny squealed loudly.

"All right," Carmie said, standing beside her. She used her hand as a visor over her eyes so she could get a good look at the water.

"Finally," the boy on the sand mumbled. Then he looked toward the food truck. "Oh, come on, brah," he said to himself. "We're never going to get up with all those guys."

"Oh, wow," Carmie said, delighted. "Here come the waves!"

"Go down there with me?" Jenny asked Carmie. Carmie looked at her mother. She seemed to be feeling okay now, but what if in another minute she got tired and weak and she was all alone?

"Is it okay, Mommy?" Carmie asked.

"Is it?" Elaine said, still looking at the water. It was as if she hadn't even heard Carmie. Then she looked at the board. "Did that boy say we could use the board?"

"We don't need that to go down there," Carmie said, trying not to sound angry. "We're not going in the water."

"Okay," Elaine said softly.

Carmie and Jenny ran across the sand toward the water.

"Hot feet!" Jenny called out, as if she was warning the people who passed by.

"Hot feet!" Carmie followed her, laughing. Just then Carmie heard voices behind her.

"Hey, check it out," a boy said.

"Hey, lady! Where you going? You could get hurt."

Carmie looked around to see what was going on. An older woman was running toward the shore, partially blocked from Carmie's view by the surfboard under her arm. She ran right past Carmie and Jenny.

"Go for it." Carmie heard a boy laugh. "Go for it, Grandma Gidget!"

The woman waved her free arm in the air, and Carmie could see its flab flapping from her blue bathing suit.

"Oh my God." Carmie stopped in her hot tracks. "Mommy!"

Chapter 7

"Elaine!" Jenny called.

"Mommy." Carmie followed her mother. "Where are you *going*?"

But Elaine didn't seem to hear her. She ran into the water, lifting her feet high as if she was running on hot coals. Carmie's legs felt roasting hot in her jeans. She hoped she was just in a bad dream where her mother looked even more ridiculous to her than usual.

"Elaine!" Jenny called again.

"What's the matter with her?" Carmie asked softly.

"She's surfing," Jenny squealed. "I can't believe you didn't tell me!"

"Tell you what?" Carmie asked. "I didn't know she was going to go out there!"

"What's the worst that can happen?" Jenny asked, throwing out her hands. "At least she knows how to swim. I hope Jon isn't too in love with his surfboard." She laughed.

"I hope you're not too in love with getting a ride home,"

Carmie said. "What if something happens to her out there?"

Jenny looked at Carmie as if reality was just starting to register. Then she turned and saw Jon running toward them with the food.

"My hot dog," Jenny cheered. "I'll be right back. Don't be a worrywart, Carm." Then she headed up the beach. Carmie stood alone and watched her mother drop the board into the water. She couldn't believe this was happening. Her mother got on top of the board on her stomach and paddled. Her white arms looked strong. The foamy tail end of a wave came rolling toward her, and Carmie watched her mother glide to its top on the board. Carmie's heart sank until she saw her mother's head again on the other side of the baby wave, closer to the surfers.

Carmie saw a lifeguard walking toward her.

"Excuse me." Carmie stopped him.

The lifeguard looked right into her eyes so she could see how gorgeous he was even though he was probably old enough to be in college.

"That's my mother." Carmie pointed.

The lifeguard looked out at the water.

"Where?" he asked.

"See?" Carmie pointed again. "She's the only mother out there. With the blue bathing suit."

"Okay." The lifeguard smiled. "So how can I help you?"

"That's not her surfboard," Carmie said.

"Does your mother know how to surf?" the lifeguard asked. "I don't want to see her get hurt."

"No, she doesn't," Carmie said. "And I'm worried about her being out there. She's sick a lot."

The lifeguard looked at the ocean. "Oh, I don't think you need to worry about her, miss," he said, staring ahead. "She looks all right to me!"

Carmie saw her mother standing up on the board. She was the first one, leading the way down the wave. Two surfers in black wet suits struggled to stay up on the wave beside her. Elaine stepped forward on the board as if she was stepping ahead of the wave. She raised her arms above her head as if she had just won the Olympics. Then she toppled into the foamy whitewater.

"Whoa!" Carmie said softly.

"Well, that was rippin'!" the lifeguard said with a laugh as he started to walk away. "Okay, so I get it. You were just making a joke. You know your mom is a surfer. So you got me. But don't do it again. I'm out here to save lives."

Elaine walked through the shallow water to catch up with the surfboard, shaking her head to get the water off. A couple of surfer girls in bikinis headed out with their boards and passed Elaine, saying something to her. Carmie was afraid that maybe they were yelling at her. Then she saw her mother give each of them a high five. She had never seen her mother give a high five in her life, and now she'd seen her mother give two in five seconds.

Jenny and Jon ran down to Carmie.

"What the—!" Jon said. "That lady's on my new board?"

"You shouldn't be mad at Jenny," Carmie said. "It's not her fault. It's my mother's. I promise you, if she ruined your surfboard at all, my mom will fix it or else she'll get you a brand-new one."

Jon looked at Jenny as if he was trying to think fast, and then he looked back at the ocean. He pretended to bonk Jenny on the top of her head. "Okay," he said. "I get it. Nice. You girls aren't from the Val; you're really locals."

"Correct again, dude." Jenny laughed. "We're going to Malibu High. Carmie's mom was really born here."

Carmie thought Jenny's story sounded as if it could be true. She watched her mother walk out of the water. The board was tucked perfectly under her arm.

"Elaine, that was so hot!" Jenny hugged her. "My mom couldn't do that in a million years!"

Elaine stuck the board into the sand and gave Jenny a hug. Then she put her arm around Carmie and kissed her on the head.

"You're like ice!" Carmie squealed. She jumped back. "Aren't you cold?"

"That felt great!" Elaine said. She held the board in front of her, inspecting it. "This your stick?" she asked Jon.

"Stick?" Jon asked. "Yes, ma'am."

"I heard you say we could take it if we couldn't help ourselves. And I'm sorry." Elaine laughed. "But I couldn't help myself!"

"It's all right," John said, hoisting the board under his arm.

"This is Carmie's mother." Jenny knocked lightly on the surfboard to get his attention.

"Hello." Jon smiled.

"Like I said, Jon," Carmie said, "if anything is broken, we can replace it."

"I guess she didn't eat it or anything," Jon said, looking at the board. Then he looked at Carmie.

Carmie tried to look at the board as if she knew what she was looking for.

"Oh, sweetie," Elaine said to Carmie. "I'm sorry if I frightened you. And, Jon, I hope you know I would never take your stick out there without knowing a little about what I was doing." Elaine laughed. "I'm not a crazy person."

"That's cool." Jon smiled. He and Elaine nodded at each other as if they shared a secret code.

"Thanks," Elaine said. "I haven't been out there for a very long time. I'm stoked!"

"Yeah." Jon chuckled to himself. "Stoked." Then he took Jenny's hot dog from her and shoved what was left of it into his mouth.

"Hey, you pig," Jenny grunted. "Give me that back. That's mine!"

"You didn't want that," Jon said, chuckling. "It will make you fat."

Carmie cringed. She pulled in her stomach. She worried that Jon was really thinking, "It will make you fat. Like Carmie."

"Besides," Jon said, "just watch me and I'll get you another one."

"Oh, *goody*," Jenny squealed, as if she really meant it.

Jon ran into the water with his board. He did it almost the same way as Carmie's mother had: running and lifting his legs high, as if he was in a marching band.

Carmie and her mother headed up the sand. Carmie knew that people were looking at them, trying to figure out who her mother was.

"Nice ride, Mom," Carmie said loudly.

"I'm a little amazed myself." Elaine laughed. She didn't sound the same to Carmie. She didn't sound like anybody's mother, much less Carmie's.

"Hey, wait for me," Jenny called out. She ran up the sand, laughing. "After you've watched once, it's kind of a snore."

Three girls on blankets propped themselves on their elbows.

"Aren't you supposed to be watching for Jon?" Carmie called.

"I did already," Jenny said. "Boys are such big babies. 'Watch me! Watch me!'" she mimicked. "They're all just out there crashing into each other. But girls rock!"

"Yeah," Carmie said.

"I guess," Elaine said.

"Are you kidding?" Jenny asked. "That was the coolest thing. You were the best one out there."

"Oh no." Elaine laughed.

"I guess, Mom." Carmie tried to laugh. "Plus, you were definitely the oldest."

"That's for sure," Elaine said. She took a peanut butter sandwich from the cooler. "Hungry, girls?"

"Isn't this so much fun?" Jenny grabbed a sandwich, took

a bite and smiled big, so Carmie could see the peanut butter on her teeth. "Fun in the sun."

"Fun in the sun," Elaine agreed with a smile. Then she lay down under the umbrella.

"Fun in the sun." Carmie laughed. She rolled up the wet legs of her jeans.

"Don't you think we should come here every day, Carm?" Jenny asked.

"I once did," Elaine said softly.

"What?" Carmie asked.

"When?" Jenny asked. "When you were in high school?"

"Maybe a little older." Elaine thought it over. "But before I became this one's mother."

Elaine reached her arm toward Carmie. Carmie couldn't believe that this was her mother. She could not imagine her mother coming to Malibu. She had thought her mom just used to play with Aunt Raleigh in the Valley, where they grew up. Her mother had told her once that she had been one of the stars in their senior musical, called *West Side Story*. But that was all. It was hard enough for Carmie to imagine her mother even being alive before she was born. Now she was supposed to swallow this?

Chapter 8

A SUPERSTAR OF MALIBU
By Carmie Hoffman

NEW SCENE:
Outside. Day. The beach. A beautiful fifteen-year-old blond girl,
CARMIE, walks down the sand with her boyfriend, DUSTY, the
lifeguard. It is a windy day today, so Dusty lets Carmie wear his
lifeguard jacket. He reaches for Carmie's hand and they run
down the beach. The waves begin to crash. They are enormous.
Dusty has to go quickly up his lifeguard tower.

DUSTY
Here, darlin'. Use these binoculars.

Carmie stands on the shore with the binoculars. She looks at the
ocean. She thinks she sees something horrible looking, like a
monster, in the water. She also spots boys in the water.

SURFERS
Run for your lives, dudes!

Carmie looks again. It is a monster. A monster of the sea. The sea monster starts walking in the water. Carmie sees the monster's face. It is like the monster is looking her right back in the eye.

CARMIE
(to herself)
Gross! Look at that thing! She must be a thousand years old!

Carmie closed her notebook. It was hard to write in the car, especially in the canyon, with all the turns. Carmie was afraid that her mother had gotten too tired at the beach and would run the car right off the road. She looked at Jenny, who was leaning against the window asleep with her mouth open.

"Are you okay up there, Mommy?" Carmie asked.

Carmie's mom had on talk radio. The man on the program kept saying, "CALL 1-800-ASK-PAUL WITH YOUR QUESTIONS. THE SWITCHBOARDS ARE LIGHTING UP. THAT'S 1-800-ASK-PAUL."

Carmie wondered why her mother was listening to people's stupid questions when she should be giving some answers to her own daughter. The road started down toward the Valley. Elaine put her foot on the brake pedal and then took it off.

"Are you okay, Mommy?" Carmie asked again.

Jenny opened her eyes. "Are we still in Malibu?"

"Not." Carmie smiled.

"We should go back tomorrow," Jenny said. "We should go every day." She sounded so excited, Carmie wondered whether she hadn't just been completely asleep. "Or at least until I have to go with my mom and dad to Colorado. Wouldn't that be cool, Carmie?"

"Oh, yeah." Carmie pretended to mean it. "Mommy," she said. "How did you learn to surf like that? Did Daddy teach you?"

"Not exactly," Elaine said. "It was just before I met your father. Some other boy taught me."

For a moment, Carmie felt carsick. She couldn't imagine her mother with anyone besides her father.

"THAT'S 1-800-ASK-PAUL," the voice said again too loudly on the radio. "NO QUESTION TOO STUPID. DON'T BE SHY. BELIEVE ME. PAUL'S HEARD IT ALL."

* * *

"So call me as soon as you ask," Jenny said to Carmie on the phone just after suppertime.

"Okay," Carmie said. "But I'm telling you, she's not going to take us back tomorrow. She'll be too tired. Trust me. Besides, what's the big deal about going back already tomorrow?"

"Because," Jenny said. "Don't you want to have fun? Face it. This day was the coolest part of our entire summer. By the time I come back from Colorado, we'll be in school already. Besides, I told Jon we'd probably come back. He's funny."

"Funny?" Carmie asked. "Now, that is funny."

"Well, he's not as funny as you," Jenny said.

"But is he cuter than me? I'm batting my eyelashes."

"Only his arms." Jenny laughed. "Besides, he likes you."

"Me?" Carmie said. "Right. I don't think so."

"You know he likes you," Jenny said. "He thinks you're funny. Besides, it's not like there's not another thousand cute guys out there. What are we going to do around here tomorrow? Sweat to death? Jon would probably let your mom even borrow his board again tomorrow. Don't you want to see your mom hang ten again?"

"I don't think so," Carmie said.

"I do," Jenny said. "That was the funniest thing. I would die if my mother could do that. Don't you want your mom to be happy again? Pleeez? She's like a dolphin. Just ask her!"

Carmie hung up the phone. She walked into the kitchen. The dishes from dinner were still in the sink. Tonight Carmie had called out for a pizza. Fluff Bucket jumped onto the counter and climbed into the pizza box.

"You really don't want that," Carmie said, swiping the last piece. "It will just make you fat."

Carmie took a bite. Jenny was right. Her mother was happier in the water. But why hadn't she ever told Carmie she could do that? Had she never told Carmie because she didn't want to have to teach her, because she thought Carmie would never be coordinated enough to learn? Why did her mother always seem sick—except for today, anyway? What if her mother had had a real life at the beach and she had given that up because Carmie was born? Who was the boy who taught her how to surf? What if she was supposed to be a pro surfer? Was having Carmie what made her mom so boring? Was that the real reason her father moved away?

Carmie finished the last bite of pizza. She was going to ask her mom a question. But it wasn't going to be whether she would take Carmie and Jenny back to the beach. It was, who are you? How come her mother never wanted to go to Malibu Beach before?

Carmie knew that her mom had been talking on the phone with Aunt Raleigh. Now Elaine's door was half closed. It was never closed. Carmie needed some real answers. She didn't even know if she could ask her mother.

"Mommy?" Carmie said. She opened the door slowly. Her mother was asleep. A strand of hair had fallen over her eye. The tip of her nose was rosy from the sun. Carmie watched her mother sleep, as she had so many times before. For the first time, she thought her mother looked almost pretty.

Carmie walked into the kitchen. She didn't know what to do now. It was too early to go to bed. Fluff Bucket followed her down the hall to the closet where the old vacuum cleaner and wrapping paper were stored. The only other things in that closet were boxes. Carmie's mother had said not to go through those boxes, because all that was in them were old things. Now Carmie wondered what those "old things" were. Her mother had said she wanted to keep the boxes sealed. But why? What if the "junk" her mother said was in there was really the answer to big questions? What else was her mother hiding from her?

Carmie pulled the top box out of the closet as quietly as she could. There was no tape across it, just a sticker that said CLOTHES. Carmie opened the flaps carefully. Her old bathing suit from when she was eight was on top. The next box was marked BOOKS and the next OLD RECORDS, and it had no tape on it. When Carmie got to the box all the way in the back, her heart skipped. The box had tape on it, but no label. She listened in the hallway. Her mother didn't stir.

"I'm doing this for your own good," Carmie said, lifting Fluff Bucket off the top of the box. She pulled up the tape and opened the first flap. On top was a small worn-out-looking black rubber vest like the ones the guys had been wearing that day at Malibu. There was a pair of old madras flip-flops that were obviously for girls. But there was nothing in the box that her father could ever have worn. Carmie looked deeper in the box, careful to memorize where everything had to be put back. She would worry about the tape later. There was a *Surfer Magazine* from 1981, and something framed. It looked like a picture of somebody who was supposed to be famous. On the corner of the picture was scribbled *For Elaine*. It was signed *Dick Dale. King of the Surf Guitar*. Did celebrities really look as old-fashioned back then as this Dick Dale guy did now? Then Carmie saw a tightly sealed envelope with her mother's handwriting on it. It said *My Love*. Carmie stopped. She knew she shouldn't look further. But if what was inside was about her father, she had a right. What would it be like to see pictures of him when he was really young? Sometimes she could hardly remember what he looked like now.

Carmie slipped open the envelope. The first picture was of Aunt Raleigh on the beach. Carmie laughed at her poufy hairdo and groovy bathing suit. More pictures of Aunt

Raleigh. One of Mom and Aunt Raleigh together, sticking their tongues out, and then one that made Carmie stop. It was a photo of a tall boy with blond hair. He had on surfer trunks and no shirt. His legs looked perfect. His chest and arms were big and handsome. A really tall surfboard was standing in the sand beside him. He had his arm around the surfboard as if it was his girlfriend. Carmie turned the picture over. On the other side it said *Moondoggie*. There was another picture of "Moondoggie" sitting on the sand with his legs crossed, and then a picture that made Carmie's heart stop. By the boy's side, instead of the surfboard, was Carmie's mom. He had his arm around her. She seemed to be smiling right at Carmie. In the next picture, they were kissing quickly, like friends. And in the next picture, they were still kissing, but not like friends anymore. On the back of that picture was written in her mother's handwriting, *Moondoggie. The Man of My Dreams. My Hero. My Future Husband. 1978.*

Carmie looked Moondoggie right in the eye. The man looked back at her as if to say, "Yeah, kid. Now you're starting to put it all together. I'm the one your mother really loved."

Moondoggie was definitely *not* her father.

Chapter 9

"Wake up!" Carmie felt something tugging on her feet.

She opened one eye. Sun was rushing into her room. Jenny was sitting on the end of her bed. On Jenny's head was a straw hat that was too big.

"What time is it?" Carmie stretched her arms.

"It's nine-thirty already," Jenny said. "Wake up! What are you, a bear?"

"What are you supposed to be with that hat?" Carmie asked. "A scarecrow?"

"No." Jenny pulled the hat over her eyes. "Wake up. We're going to Malibu. And I am Malibu Jenny."

"Well, I don't think I'm Malibu Carmie. Are you kidding? My mother won't take us again." Carmie pulled the sheets over her face. "She's not feeling good. I already asked her last night."

"No, you didn't, my little liar." Jenny laughed. "But I knew you wouldn't. So I came over early this morning to ask Elaine myself."

"No, you didn't." Carmie sat straight up.

"Serious," Jenny said, as if she was telling Carmie she had just won a thousand dollars. "Your mom said if you wake up before I have to leave for Colorado, we can still go. She's already ready."

"No, she isn't," Carmie said. "Oh, right. I almost forgot. Today is April Fools' Day."

* * *

Carmie leaned against Jenny in the backseat of their old station wagon.

"What time did you go to sleep last night, Carmie?" her mother asked. Her voice sounded as if she had a lot of energy.

"I don't remember," Carmie said. She tried her hardest to sound awake. "Not too late."

For a moment Carmie thought maybe she was really still asleep and this was just a dream. A dream in which her mother was suddenly wide awake and loving to drive to the beach for the second day in a row.

"Isn't this the most perfect June day?" Elaine asked as they started down the canyon.

"I know," Jenny said. She bounced up and down in the seat. Her big hat smashed against the ceiling.

"It's okay." Carmie laughed. "Almost as beautiful as the park pool."

Elaine turned on the AM radio and flipped through the talk stations. "Let's find the surf report," she said.

"How do you know where that station is, Mommy?" Carmie asked.

"Are you going to surf again today?" Jenny asked. "I bet Jon would probably let you use his surfboard. Can you teach us how to do that? Will you?"

Carmie cringed. She didn't want her mother teaching her how to surf. How humiliating would that be? Carmie wasn't even that good a swimmer.

"Quite frankly, Jenny, I'm a little run-down today," Elaine said. "I wouldn't know how to teach you. Believe me. Yesterday was a fluke. I'm just good for bringing you girls back here for one more day."

Carmie felt relieved and suddenly happier. In a few hours they would be back home and things could get back to normal. She could live through this.

"I think the parking lot is right up ahead, Mommy," Carmie said.

"I remember." Elaine smiled. "Don't worry, Carmie. I didn't forget."

Elaine made a left turn off the Pacific Coast Highway. The lot was filled with Mustangs and little convertibles. Boys in wet suits were walking toward the beach, looking like perfect blond seals. The beautiful Malibu girls in their bikinis were everywhere. A few of them had on wet suit tops with little bikini bottoms. Their hair was wet and straight. The ocean air was already making Carmie's hair frizzy. She tried to straighten it with her hand. Then she reached into her bag to make sure she still had her cell phone.

"Cool," Jenny squealed out her window. "The sun feels so good here. You can smell the ocean. This is so much better than Van Nuys!"

Two girls in perfect matching purple bikinis turned and looked at the car.

"Vals," Carmie heard one girl say as they passed. Her voice sounded disgusted.

"I thought you were a beach girl," Carmie said.

"I am!" Jenny laughed. She tipped her straw hat. "I'm Malibu Jenny."

"Then the whole beach doesn't have to know we live in the Valley, do they?" Carmie forced a laugh.

"Why not?" Jenny looked at Carmie. "We do, don't we?"

"Yeah, I suppose," Carmie said. "But just for this last day I have an idea. Let's at least pretend we live in Beverly Hills."

"We're the girls from *The B.H.*" Jenny laughed. She tipped her hat again. "We are rich, rich, rich and famous. Whatever."

Carmie and Jenny carried the cooler onto the sand. Elaine followed. "Pick a spot," Jenny said.

"I'm keeping my eye out for Jon," Carmie said loudly enough that the girls they passed on the sand would hear. "He's probably in the same place we see him every day. Unless he has to work today on that *B.H.* show."

Carmie saw that a girl with strawberry blond hair was listening to her. She was definitely a Malibu girl, even though her hair was semi-stringy. Carmie thought the girl must know that Carmie was somebody important. Carmie was an original. Carmie was wearing blue jeans because she had a style of her own.

"Isn't this the coolest place?" Jenny looked all around. She put her hand on her head to make sure the wind wasn't blowing her hat off. "I just love it here. Thank you so much for bringing us back, Elaine. How's here?" she called back. "Here's a spot."

Carmie and Jenny opened their big beach towels. Carmie lifted her face to the sun. She felt as if the sun was looking back at just her and smiling. It was saying, "You belong here. And so does your mother." Carmie lay down on her towel. The waves were breaking already today. The sound was peaceful, even with the surfers hooting far out in the ocean.

"This is awesome, Carm." Jenny patted Carmie's leg. Carmie turned onto her stomach, watching her mom open the umbrella. Elaine seemed very tired again.

"I'm just going to take a little snooze," Elaine said. "You want me to put some suntan lotion on you first, sweetie? I don't want you to burn."

"Okay," Carmie said. She looked at the next blanket to see if anybody was watching.

Carmie thought of the pictures from the night before. She thought of her dad and then that man Moondoggie. What kind of a stupid name was that? What was his real name, anyway? What if her mom had really been supposed to marry him? Then maybe Carmie would have been born at the beach. What if what Jenny had told Jon the day before as a joke was really the truth? That she really did belong here. She should have been born in Malibu. Her mother's cool fingers with the cream felt great on her hot back. Today her fingers felt stronger, as if they held the answers to many secrets.

"Here we are in Malibu." Jenny laughed. "Mali-boo-boo.

Come on, Carmie. You want to go down to the water with me? Can we, Elaine?"

Carmie looked around to make sure nobody could hear they had to get permission from her mother.

"Go ahead," Carmie's mother said. "Just remember this is a surfing beach. Those are surfers out there. Those boards are going fast and they can be dangerous."

Jenny took off her big hat. She stepped out of her shorts. Carmie saw the girls on the next towels checking out Jenny's body.

"Aren't you going to take off those jeans?" Jenny asked.

"Maybe later," Carmie said. "It's not that hot yet."

Jenny led the way.

"Call emergency makeover," Carmie heard one of the girls say. She could tell they were talking about her.

"Wait up, Jenny," Carmie said. Jenny stopped. Carmie ran back to her mother. She picked up her towel and wrapped it around her waist. Then she took off her jeans as fast as she could without letting the towel fall.

"You sure you're going to be okay alone here, Mommy?" Carmie asked.

"Of course. Why wouldn't I be?" Elaine asked. She sounded a little more awake. "I'm just going to fall asleep. If anything, I may take a little walk on the sand."

"Cool," Carmie said. She looked at her mother. Why had she ever made fun of her? For a moment Carmie felt as if she might cry. She thought it must be sad to be an older person, like her mother, and to have to be around all the young people. Then Carmie checked that her towel was tight around her waist.

60

"Come on," Jenny called to Carmie. "Surf's up. Let's roll!"

"Carmie, your thongs!" Elaine called out.

Carmie stepped through the sand barefoot as if her feet were on fire. The shore and the nice cold water looked too far away. Carmie just kept her eyes on them. Today nobody was sitting out there waiting. The surfers were standing on their boards. There were a hundred of them crowding to ride the same waves.

"Those guys are so cool," Carmie called to Jenny.

"No, they're hot!" Jenny laughed.

"Well, they're not as hot as my feet," Carmie said. "They're on fire!"

"Carmie, you are the most fun girl in Beverly Hills." Jenny laughed.

The foamy ends of the waves rolled onto the shore and between Carmie's toes. She checked and tightened her towel.

"And these guys are ridiculous," Jenny said. "Look at them. They look like clowns!"

Carmie laughed, watching some of the guys lose their balance and fly into the water. She thought of her mother out there the day before and how somehow she had been able to keep standing on the wave.

"Well, one of those clowns is probably your dream boy," Carmie said.

"Make that nightmare." Jenny laughed. She shielded her eyes with her hands to get a look.

Carmie knew it wouldn't be long before Jenny spotted Jon, and then he'd come out of the water and they'd want to be by themselves. Jenny always seemed to forget Carmie as soon as she met a new boy. For a second Carmie thought maybe one of those Malibu boys out there that day would like her, too. Not Jon, of course. She wasn't pretty enough. Besides, what good would it be to have a boyfriend if Carmie could only see him two days a year? She breathed in the ocean air. She looked up. The sun was smiling at her again. It could happen.

"All right, surfers," Jenny called out. "Lookin' good. Lookin' good!"

Just then Jon came out of the water. His wet blond hair looked darker and was matted around his eyes. His surfboard was under his arm. He smiled, blue eyes twinkling in the sun. His dimples looked huge.

"Hey," Jon said to Jenny. "You came back to find me!"

"Of course, dude," Jenny teased. "Just to watch you and all those other cute guys out there."

"Right." Jon shook his head like a wet dog in Jenny's face.

"Liquid!" Jenny yelped.

"Did you see me out there?" Jon asked, looking back at the water. "I almost got pounded. But I was cool. There were some really crankin' barrels."

"Right, dude." Jenny laughed. Jon put his arm around her waist and pulled her close, as if he was going to kiss her.

"Hey, Jon," a Malibu girl said, passing them on the sand. She had short brown hair and a magazine-model body. "Nice job out there."

"Thanks, Beth," Jon said, waving to her.

Carmie pretended she was looking for someone in the

water. "Hey," she said, trying to get Jenny's attention. "I'll see ya back up there."

"No, stay with us," Jenny said, pretending to try to push Jon away from her.

"Yeah," Jon said, laughing.

"That's okay," Carmie said. "I've got to go sharpen my pencil."

She headed up the beach. She checked her towel. She thought of what she had just said. Where had that come from? She wondered if she could have said anything lamer. What difference did it make? Had Jenny even heard what she'd said? She would have known that Carmie didn't even have a pencil. And who was Beth? Couldn't Jenny see that Jon already had a girlfriend? Did Jenny really think Jon was going to give up his girlfriend, who was a real Malibu girl, just because Jenny had big breasts? Couldn't Jenny see they didn't belong here? As she walked, to keep herself from crying, Carmie thought of what she would write as soon as she got back to the towel.

SUPERSTAR OF THE CENTURY HITS THE SUN
By Carmie Hoffman

Daytime. Beach. It is a perfect day at Malibu Beach. It's packed, but one section of the beach is the most packed. That is because that is where the famous scriptwriter CARMIE HOFFMAN, nineteen, is sitting.

JENNY
Oh please, Carmie. Can't I get your autograph first? Don't you remember me? I'll do anything to be your friend again.

Carmie's feet started to burn. She had to get through the maze of sunbathers as fast as she could without kicking sand in anybody's face. She held on to her towel tightly. She could hardly wait to get back to her spot. For the first time, she was glad her mother was up there waiting for her. Carmie didn't want to be alone now. Her mother would understand even though Carmie would never tell her how she felt. And Carmie's mother would be happy to go home, just as Carmie would be. Carmie didn't remember their things being so far away. She thought their spot should be easy to see, since the other people on the beach weren't there with their mothers. Then Carmie saw the red and white top of an umbrella. She sighed. She was tired, but her feet ran faster. In a minute she would be at her own towel beside her mother.

For a second Carmie felt as if her heart had stopped. She could see the whole umbrella now. Maybe she had the wrong umbrella. Her mother wasn't asleep under it. Her mother wasn't anywhere.

Chapter 10

Carmie jumped into her jeans. Where had her mother gone? Whose board could she be on today? Jon was already on his. And besides, her mother's purse was gone. Nobody had taken Carmie's backpack. What if someone had taken her mother and her purse? What if she had just gone off herself into the ocean, only this time she was too tired even to swim?

Carmie sat on Jenny's towel. She reached for her cell phone. She pretended to check whether anybody had called. Then she took out her notebook. There was no reason to panic.

SUPER SURFER STAR OF THE CENTURY
By Carmie Hoffman

Daytime. Malibu Beach. It is a perfect day at Malibu Beach. It's crowded. But the most crowded spot is by one blanket. That is where famous scriptwriter CARMIE HOFFMAN, age nineteen, is sitting under an umbrella. She is signing autographs. Carmie is wearing a perfect white bathing suit under a dazzling white cover-up. JENNY and JON are trying to go to the front of the autograph line.

JENNY

Carmie, please! Let me have cuts! Don't you remember? I'm your best friend.

JON

I am not into autographs. But this one I know is going to be worth something, man. If you just give me one page with your name on it, I'll leave Jenny alone. Believe me. It's no big deal. I'll even go back with my real girlfriend. And she's not as funny as you.

Carmie gazed all around. Nobody looked anything like her mother. Carmie put on her flip-flops. She didn't know which way to walk first. If anything happened to her mother, Carmie would never forgive Jenny for being so selfish and making her mother come back to Malibu again that day in the first place.

Finally she started walking away from where Jenny was. A lifeguard was sitting high up in his chair. Carmie couldn't tell if he was the same lifeguard as the day before, but she wasn't going to find out. She tried to imagine her mother and Aunt Raleigh and that Moondoggie guy sitting on this beach, but she couldn't. Carmie wondered if the people she passed had seen her mother surfing the day before. Would they recognize Carmie and know that even though she didn't look like it, she was somebody important?

Carmie looked at her cell as if she was checking for messages. Nobody ever called her except Aunt Raleigh and her father. Suddenly Carmie felt as if she might start to cry. If her father had been here, her mother wouldn't have wandered off like this. If they were still married, she'd be healthy all the time and not tired. Maybe she'd even be happy. If he was at the beach and not in Indiana.

Carmie saw the last lifeguard stand. She couldn't pass this one by. She walked to the edge of the big white chair. High above her, the lifeguard was looking out at the ocean. Carmie could see the pier and the end of the beach. Hardly anybody had a towel spread out there.

"Excuse me," Carmie called up.

Just then she saw something close to the shore. It was a beach blanket covered with people, but they were not like the other people on the beach. A really tall surfboard stood in the sand beside them, bigger and older than any surfboard Carmie had seen. The people were laughing really loudly. They looked old and sort of raggedy, as if maybe they were homeless.

"Did you need something?" the lifeguard called, climbing out of the chair. She recognized his face.

"Hey." The lifeguard looked Carmie right in the eye. "You're the girl from yesterday. With the surfing mother. You don't have a joke for me today?"

"No," Carmie said, swallowing hard. "I know this sounds stupid and I'm really sorry to bother you again today. But I'm telling you the truth."

"So what's the problem today?" The lifeguard folded his big arms.

"I can't find her. Her purse is missing and everything, so I know she's not out surfing this time."

"Why don't you check over there?" he asked, pointing at the nearby blanket. Carmie checked that her towel was still tight around her waist. Now she knew that the lifeguard was laughing at her.

"You mean with all the homeless people?" Carmie asked, trying to laugh too.

"What homeless people?" The lifeguard looked confused. "Them?" He pointed at the blanket again. "They're not homeless! Are you kidding me? Those are legends." The lifeguard shook his head, starting back up the chair. "Check there, young lady," he called down. "They're the oldest people on the beach. Maybe they'll know something."

Carmie walked slowly toward the blanket. Could her mother be with those people? Some of them looked even older than she was. Was that why the lifeguard had called them legends? What could they want with her mother? When she got closer, Carmie saw that there were three women with long hair wearing bathing suits. Two of them had dark skin that looked leathery from being in the sun. There was a short Hawaiian-looking man who had dark hair with gray in it. He was wearing baggy trunks and holding a baby above his head. Carmie then saw that one of the women had the same blue bathing suit as her mother. She was laughing so hard, Carmie hardly recognized her face.

"Oh, sweetheart." Elaine stood up quickly. She walked over to Carmie and put her arm around her. "This is my pride and joy," Elaine announced. "This is my daughter, Carmie."

"Far out," one of the women said. "She's a beauty."

"Righteous," the Hawaiian man said. "You look just like your mom."

"Hello," Carmie said, trying to sound polite and not frightened. "Everybody usually says I look like my dad. He has dark hair."

"Well, I'm very stoked to meet you," another woman said, moving closer to shake Carmie's hand. She was as tall as the big surfboard, and she had long bangs that she kept pushing out of her face.

Carmie shook the woman's hand.

"Oh, sweetie," Elaine said. "These are my old friends from a hundred years ago."

Everyone laughed. Carmie had never seen her mother tell a joke that people actually thought was funny. She had never seen her mother with many friends. Mostly the only adults she had seen her mother with since the divorce were Aunt Raleigh and Uncle Roy. What was happening to Carmie's life? Had her mother gotten so weird now that she could just run into the ocean at any moment and then make best friends with old homeless people? Was that what the lifeguard had meant by "legends"? Was a legend in surfspeak the same thing as a homeless fossil?

"Oh, I'm sorry, sweetie," Elaine said. "Were you frightened? Were you looking for me?"

"Only everywhere," Carmie said.

Everybody laughed. Carmie tried not to smile.

"I just went for a little stroll," Elaine said. "I didn't think I would run into these guys here! This is Candy, once known as Candy the Cotton Candy Rip Curler."

"Hey," Candy said, smiling.

"And this is the famous Aloha Fats."

The Hawaiian man lifted the baby onto his shoulders. "And this is Baby Kuana. Your mother hasn't known him for quite a hundred years yet."

Everybody laughed as if that was the funniest joke they had ever heard. A man with faded blond hair had been sitting beside Carmie's mother on the blanket. "Hey, Carmie." He smiled. Carmie saw he had big dimples and almost perfect teeth. "How old are you?"

"Thirteen," Carmie said, trying not to look anyone in the eye. "Next month I'm fourteen."

The man looked at Elaine and they smiled at each other. Carmie had never seen her mother look at a man like that—well, not since her father.

"This is Sean, sweetie," Carmie's mother said.

Sean looked right at Carmie and she saw he was still handsome. He got up to shake her hand, laughing.

"I'm also known as Moondoggie."

Suddenly Carmie felt a cold chill run down her back.

She looked at her mother. "I'll be right back," she said.

"Why?" Elaine asked. "Wait just another minute, sweetheart. I'll come with you."

"That's okay," Carmie said, checking her towel. "I just remembered. I left Jenny alone with our stuff. I told her I'd be right back."

Carmie started to run through the sand. This time it was harder because she didn't know now what she was trying to run away from or what she had left to run back to.

Chapter 11

Carmie headed up the sand. It seemed as if every radio on the beach played the same oldies station.

"This is for all of you," the disc jockey cut in. "The cutest girls in the world. All those fine ladies out on Malibu Beach today. You know this one. It's the Beach Boys. An oldie but not a moldie. This one's a legend."

I wish they all could be California girls.

Carmie tightened her towel. All she wanted was to wake up and find that she had been dreaming in her bed, which she should never have left. Carmie knew this song. If the Beach Boys were legends and they were famous, and the lifeguard said all the old beach people were supposed to be legends, did that mean they were famous once too? Was her mother famous? That was impossible. Then why did famous people ever want to hang out with her mother? Carmie's mind went dark trying to figure it all out.

Wish they all could be California girrrrlllllssssss.

Carmie could tell that people were looking at her. That

71

song wasn't about her. She didn't belong there. She was getting off the beach as fast as she could. Jenny belonged there, because she had the body of a Malibu girl. Carmie's mom might have belonged there once too. Maybe Jenny was Elaine's real daughter and not Carmie. So where was Carmie supposed to go now? To Jenny's family instead? Would they want to take her with them to Colorado? Maybe it would have to be Aunt Raleigh and Uncle Roy. They would want her. But was she supposed to live on tofu for the rest of her life? She would have to go live with her father in Indiana. It would be horrible there, but at least Carmie wouldn't have to worry about not being pretty. The Beach Boys never wrote a song called "Indiana Girls."

Carmie felt nauseated. She needed to find Jenny. Jenny would make everything seem okay again.

At their spot, Carmie could see the umbrella, but no Jenny. What had she been thinking? Of course Jenny was still with Jon. Carmie was going to be all alone on that blanket. Her mother was still going to be with Moondoggie.

Jenny and her mother could both turn their backs on her. But Carmie didn't have to put up with it. She turned and headed back to get her mother. Jenny could stay here forever if she wanted to. But Carmie was going home.

NOTES IN MIND FOR MOVIE SCRIPT
By Carmie Hoffman

SCENE ONE:
Daytime. A beach better than Malibu Beach. Beautiful, gorgeous eighteen-year-old CARMIE sits on her towel. All the boys want to

be her boyfriend. Carmie stands up so everybody can see that in her pink wet suit (the only one on the beach), she is a perfect ten. Carmie grabs her surfboard. She runs into the water.

CARMIE
(to the fans)
Watch me. Watch me. I'm going to catch the best wave yet.

Carmie passed the pier and the lifeguard's stand. Finally she saw the big blanket. There were a few more people there now. More surfboards were stuck into the sand. Her mother was still sitting right next to Moondoggie. How had she become one of them so quickly? If Carmie was her mother's pride and joy, if Carmie was the best thing that ever happened to her mother, as her mother always said, then how come her mother had never looked as happy in Carmie's life as she did now? Carmie couldn't figure it all out.

"Oh, sweetie!" Elaine stood up from the towel. "Did you find Jenny? Are you two ready to go?"

"Yeah," Carmie said. "We're ready to go."

Carmie looked at her mother. It was as if she didn't care that she was the only one on the beach with pale white legs. She was with a man who wasn't Carmie's father, but Carmie couldn't deny he was handsome. Maybe even a little more handsome than her father, even though he did have an incredibly stupid nickname. Plus, this man might have been famous once. Carmie's mother seemed healthy now. Why would she need Carmie?

"I think Jenny's got a bad sunburn," Carmie said.

73

"Ouch," Elaine said, picking up her purse. "Okay. I'm ready."

"That sun will fry ya," Moondoggie said. "Look at me." He held out his dark leathery arm. "Takes a while for the sun to get used to you," he said, laughing. "Then it never lets you go."

Moondoggie stood up and smiled. He looked Carmie in the eye. It felt just like it had when Carmie looked at him in the old photograph the night before. It was as if he was saying, "Hey, kid. Yeah, it's me again. I'm on to you. Don't you want your mother to have fun in her life?"

"I'm so psyched I ran into all of you guys," Elaine said. Carmie cringed. She had never heard her mother use the word *psyched* before.

"It wouldn't have happened if Carmie and her friend Jenny hadn't convinced me to drive them back here today," Elaine went on.

"Then you and your friend Jenny should drag her back tomorrow," Aloha Fats said to Carmie.

"Righteous," Moondoggie said, nodding toward the ocean. "We'll get you back out there, Elaine."

Carmie's mother laughed. Carmie thought she looked almost pretty.

"Maybe next year," Elaine said, smiling at Moondoggie. "I don't want to burn my girls three days in a row."

Carmie swallowed hard. What if, when they left, her mother started looking tired and sick again? What was she going to tell her mom when she saw that Jenny didn't really have a sunburn? What difference did it make, as long as they could just go home?

74

"Hey," two voices called.

Carmie saw two Malibu girls coming up behind them in the sand. They were probably juniors or seniors in high school.

"Hey, Barb. Hey, Eva," Moondoggie said. "What brings you all the way to this side of the beach?"

"Hey, Sean," one of the girls said. "Seen Coady?"

"He's been out there for a few hours already," Sean said. "He's got to be somewhere in that circus."

"Will you tell him I said hey?" the girl asked.

"Sure, Barb. No problemo." Moondoggie looked as if he was the only adult on the planet who didn't have a problem in the world.

Carmie watched the two girls walk away. Barb looked amazing in her pink-and-lime-striped French bikini.

"Once I looked like that," Elaine sighed.

"Still do," Moondoggie said.

"All right then, sure." Elaine started to walk away. "Take it easy, everybody," she called, laughing.

"Nice to meet you, Carmie," Moondoggie said.

"Okay," Carmie said, looking down.

Then suddenly, out the corner of her eye, Carmie saw something coming toward her. It was a boy. He was probably no more than a sophomore or a junior. He was running up from the shore, carrying a surfboard. He had on a short wet suit with no sleeves. His legs were thin, but strong looking, and his arms were tanned and muscular. He was wearing glasses held by a chain around his neck. His hair was light brown, but part of it was streaked blond from the sun.

"Hey," the boy called out.

"Hey," everybody said.

"Howzit?" the boy asked, walking up to Moondoggie.

"You tell me, brah," Moondoggie said, handing the boy a towel.

"It's okay," the boy said, looking down. "Haven't you guys been out there yet?"

"Too ballistic out there right now," Aloha Fats said.

Moondoggie laughed, slapping the boy gently on the back.

"Hey, Elaine. You've got to just come back here for one second and meet my boy," Moondoggie called.

"Oh, wow, Sean." Elaine smiled. Then she turned to Carmie. "Just one last second, sweetie. Do you mind?"

Carmie followed her mother. "Oh, wow, you look just like Sean," Elaine said, smiling. She couldn't seem to stop smiling.

"Well, I don't know," Coady said, looking down.

Carmie tried not to look Coady in the eye. She hoped that maybe because he was wearing glasses in the sun it would be hard for him to see her at all.

"And, Coady," Moondoggie said, "this is my friend Elaine's daughter. This is Carmie."

"Hi." Coady stuck his surfboard deep into the sand, still looking down.

"She lives in the Valley," Moondoggie said.

"Yeah, I guess," Carmie said. "But don't hold that against me."

Everybody laughed. Even Coady smiled.

"You ever surf, Carmie?" Moondoggie asked.

"No," Carmie said. "Not in Van Nuys."

Everybody laughed again.

"It looks like it's calming down out there, man," Moondoggie said.

"It's starting to," Coady said.

Carmie had never heard anybody's father call him man before.

"Maybe you could just take Carmie out, Coady," Moondoggie said. "Let her get a feel for the motion of the ocean."

Coady shook the water out of his hair.

"You still got my contacts here?" he asked, as if he hadn't even heard what his father had just said.

Coady looked at the water. He took off his glasses. Then he looked at Carmie as if he was going to get a good look for the first time. "Yeah, I suppose," he said, smiling. "Want to?"

"Today?" Carmie felt for her towel. She was too shocked to figure out whether Coady was repulsed by her but had to do this because his dad said so, or whether he thought she was at all cute.

"Well, yeah," Coady said, laughing. He looked right at her. "This is it."

Carmie felt warm and nervous all over. Coady was just the right height, not too tall but not too short. He didn't have a dimple, but she could tell that his blue-gray eyes really meant what he said. "This is it." He wanted to take her into the water. He was perfect.

Chapter 12

*　　*　*　*

"It's okay, Mom?" Carmie asked. "You're going to be okay?"

"I'm fine, sweetie," Elaine said, setting her purse back down in the sand. "It's Jenny I'm worried about. I don't want her to get sick."

"No, she said she could wait about a half hour longer," Carmie said.

"That's cool," Moondoggie said to Coady. "A half hour. That gives you about fifteen minutes."

"Good, Elaine," Candy the Cotton Candy Rip Curler said. "So now you can open up your wallet and show us Carmie's baby pictures."

"Do you have to?" Carmie asked.

"Go on, Coady!" Moondoggie waved. "Watch," he said, reaching for Elaine's hand. "Carmie will get hooked. Just like her mother."

"Not that hooked." Elaine laughed and looked deep into Moondoggie's eyes. Carmie didn't like having to figure out the secret code in her mother's sentences.

"All right," Coady said, looking as if he didn't care what his father was talking about.

"Have fun," Elaine said.

"Go for it!" Moondoggie called.

Carmie followed Coady over the sand. If she hadn't just made up that lie about Jenny, she could have gotten this over with in one minute and left before anything too humiliating happened. She looked at the cranberry stripes on Coady's surfboard turning and twisting. His calf muscles shone in the sun like perfect bulbs. The sound of the ocean was everywhere.

"I like your surfboard," Carmie said. "I think it's probably the best-looking one I've seen out here all day."

"Oh," Coady said, as if he never thought about whether his was the best or the worst.

"It's really nice of you to do this for me," Carmie said, trying to think quickly of something to say. "I know what it feels like to have your parents make you do something you don't want to do." She laughed as if she was making a joke.

"It's okay," Coady said. Then he stopped. "Besides"—he looked at Carmie—"my father never makes me do anything." His voice was serious. Carmie felt frightened. Was he mad at her?

"You're lucky!" She tried to laugh.

"Yeah, maybe," Coady said. Carmie could see him smiling. He started walking. She felt better. Coady was saying he was doing this because he wanted to. It made Carmie feel warm inside. Was this a dream? Did Coady know the secret about their parents? Or was this just what it felt like

79

to have a surfer boyfriend? A shy boy whom Barb and probably lots of other girls wanted, but he wanted Carmie. He liked her because she was different from all the others. Better. The sun shimmied on the horizon. The waves were turning into small tubes of perfect fluffy foam. Seagulls circled overhead and cawed. Now all Carmie had to do was go into the water.

"I'm sort of new at this," Carmie said. "I'm like a freshman out here."

"First time in the ocean?" Coady asked.

"No," Carmie said. "I've been in Santa Monica. But I'm not the world's greatest swimmer. I'm better in the pool."

Her feet felt the cold rocks of the ocean floor. She didn't want to go another step. If she kept walking, the water would catch up to the towel. She couldn't take off her towel.

"Do you want me to just watch you?" Carmie asked.

"If you want," Coady said softly. "But it's not like there's going to be much to see." He looked at Carmie. She felt embarrassed. He looked at her as if he was seeing something. Was he seeing that she was not much to see?

"What year are you in?" Carmie asked.

"This is so righteous," Coady said, as if he had never heard the word *school* before. "Even when there're no waves." He hoisted his surfboard under his arm. Then he walked farther out.

Carmie followed. "Yikes!" She lifted her feet as if she was in a marching band. "Ice!" She tried to laugh like she was laid back.

"Want to know the best way to warm up fast?" Coady asked.

"What?" Carmie asked, afraid to hear the answer.

"It's probably just like in a pool," Coady said. "Just dive in." He disappeared into the water. A second later he bobbed back up. His glasses were still on the chain. He shook his hair. His bangs were matted on his forehead like seaweed. Carmie froze and looked at her towel.

"I got a bad burn on my legs already today," she said quickly. "I'd better keep this on."

"Just dunk once," Coady said, as if he hadn't even heard what Carmie had just said.

"Okay," Carmie said. She closed her eyes. She disappeared. Then the sound of the ocean was everything.

"Yikes!" She jumped back up. Her body knew there was no place to go. She was trapped in the shock. All she could feel was her towel trying to pull her by the waist back down to the ocean floor.

"That wasn't too bad." Carmie laughed.

"Great. One more time ought to do it," Coady said, dropping into the water up to his shoulders. "After that you won't feel a thing."

"Okay," Carmie said. She was too cold to stop herself.

"Yeow!" She bobbed back up. "I now officially have frostbite."

"What's that?" Coady asked.

"Nothing important," Carmie said. "It's just something people in Indiana get." She could feel her towel ballooning around her like a lead parachute. She sat down in the water. Coady looked farther out over the ocean. He dropped his board and put his hand on the middle to steady it. "Ready?" he asked.

Carmie looked at the cranberry stripes and swirls that looked so threatening now, floating on top of the water.

"For what?" Carmie asked. "Isn't our fifteen minutes up? I'm just worried about Jenny. She's my best friend."

"I don't know," Coady said. "Maybe we still have a few minutes. You need to go back?"

"Probably should," Carmie said. "This was great. Thanks for taking me out here."

Coady turned his board toward the shore. Carmie smiled. She had been with a real surfer. Even if it had been for only fifteen minutes. She looked at Coady. Carmie could tell he was looking back at her behind his glasses. Were his eyes saying to her eyes, "I know who you are. I know who you could have been. You could have been my sister. You belong here. Now what is this I'm feeling? Our connection is so deep. Could it be love?"?

"My mom and dad are divorced." Carmie heard herself blurt the words out. Then she cringed. Why had she needed to tell him that? Was it just so he would know they might have something in common?

"Oh," Coady said. Then he got onto the board on his stomach. Carmie watched his beautiful arms paddle slowly through the flat water. She thought that didn't look so hard. He was only a few feet ahead of her. She looked into the distance. Soon she would be back with her mother in the sand. Coady turned his head to look over his shoulder. Carmie looked too. A baby wave was coming.

"Might as well take a little cruise," Coady said.

"What do you mean?" Carmie asked. Her voice sounded frightened.

"You sure you don't want a ride?" Coady asked.

"That's okay," Carmie said.

"Okay, then just jump into the wave," Coady said. His voice was soft and gentle. "It will lift you up, then set you back down."

Carmie looked behind her again. The wave coming toward her looked like an escalator going up and up. It looked as if it could go over her head.

"Just jump into it," she told herself. She practiced a jump. The towel pulled her back down. Carmie panicked. How was she ever going to get back to the shore with that thing still around her waist?

"Wait!" Carmie called. "I think I want to try."

"Cool." Coady slid off the board.

"I just lie down on this?" Carmie asked, trying to buoy her body onto the board. She jumped onto it. The board teetered back and forth. She couldn't stay on it. The towel weighed too much for the board. Any second Coady would say something.

"Here you go." Coady steadied his surfboard in the water. Then Carmie was on it on her stomach. The towel was flat and soaking. Carmie wanted to die, but it was too late for that now. Whatever Coady was thinking of her, she couldn't fix it. He could see everything. He could never think of her like bikini Barb or her friend, because Carmie was ten pounds overweight. He could never think of her as a girlfriend. But at least he could like her enough not to tell everybody how pathetic she was.

Carmie held on tightly to the sides of the board. Then she felt Coady give the back of the board a shove ahead of the wave.

"Yeoow!" Carmie squealed. She couldn't help it. She knew she wasn't going very fast, but it felt like a hundred miles an hour.

It felt great. She could see the shore and the sand coming in to meet her. The foamy bubbles got smaller and smaller until finally there was only the very shallow water to walk out of. Carmie clumsily got off the board. She looked at the sun. It was smiling down at her. Her whole body was smiling. She had done this thing.

She had gone for it.

Chapter 13

"I know it's like nothing to you," Carmie said, following Coady up the sand. "But that was the coolest thing."

"Yeah." Coady glanced back at her. His voice sounded serious again.

"At least our parents should get a laugh out of this." Carmie laughed.

"I suppose." Coady looked ahead.

Carmie cringed. Had she just said the wrong thing again?

"Hey, Carmie," Elaine called.

"Hey," Carmie called. She liked the casual way she sounded saying "hey" to her mother.

"Howzit?" Moondoggie called to Coady. "She ready for the Pipe?"

"Well, I'm not exactly ready for the Olympics," Carmie called before Coady could answer.

Everybody laughed.

"That's okay, sweetie. Neither am I." Elaine quickly picked

up her purse off the blanket. "But at least you went out there, Carmie," she said, putting her arm around Carmie.

"I guess." Carmie tried not to blush. She looked at her mother. Elaine gave Moondoggie a big smile. Carmie felt guilty. Her mother didn't look ready to go. She looked happy and awake. It was Moondoggie; he was changing everything.

"We've got to go." Elaine laughed. "This was so much fun."

"Take it easy," Aloha Fats called.

"Later," Moondoggie said.

"I bet she could be a good surfer," Coady called out. Carmie stopped. She was afraid Coady was going to finish the sentence, ". . . if she ditched the towel." Then everybody would laugh. They would all know that Coady was just making fun of her the whole time.

"You think so?" Elaine stopped. "Why do you say that?" She sounded as if she really wanted to know.

"It's a joke, Mom." Carmie pretended to laugh. Her heart was pounding. "You don't get it. Come on."

"Because she wasn't afraid," Coady called out. "She wasn't afraid to get up on that board at the crucial moment. She went for it."

"Well, it wasn't exactly me," Carmie said softly.

"That's my daughter, all right," Elaine said with a smile, taking Carmie's hand.

"You know, if she ever wanted to check it out, Elaine," Moondoggie said flirtatiously, "I'm sure Coady would be happy to take Carmie out again."

"Well, maybe next time." Elaine gave him a long smile.

"When's that?" Moondoggie laughed.

"Tomorrow?" Coady called.

Carmie turned and saw Coady smiling at her.

"Yeah, tomorrow!" Carmie laughed, too embarrassed to keep looking at him. Her heart was pounding. This was like a movie. A movie about a famous surf daughter and her mother who maybe once knew how to surf, who are now walking off into the sunset together, the best of beach-girl friends, to the other side of Malibu. While they are walking away, everybody watches. Especially one special surfer, a young, serious surfer.

The sun pounded down and Carmie could feel her calves pumping, trying to carry her and her towel through the sand.

"Those friends go so far back." Elaine squeezed Carmie's hand tightly. "Now they have kids of their own. Amazing."

"Did you really used to surf with them?" Carmie asked.

"Sure." Elaine laughed. "Your old mother was a surfer a hundred years ago. We used to come here, Aunt Raleigh and I. Gosh. These people go so far back. I almost forgot they were my friends." Carmie thought of Jenny and suddenly began to run ahead. Jenny had to know that she was supposed to be burned.

"Are you going to be okay, Mommy?" Carmie called back.

"Of course," Elaine said, smiling. "Go ahead. You girls start packing everything up."

Carmie tried to run faster.

A hundred questions flashed through her mind, but she couldn't think of a way to ask her mother any of them. Suddenly the movie stopped. Now all Carmie had to do was figure out the ending.

Finally she spotted her mother's umbrella. Jenny wasn't there. Carmie let herself breathe and count to ten. Jenny had to be somewhere down by the water with Jon still.

Carmie had gone from one side of Malibu Beach, by the pier, to the other. Surf guys were everywhere, with their boards under their arms.

Suddenly Carmie spotted Jenny walking slowly into the shallow water.

"Yo, hey!" Carmie called as loudly as she could. "Jenny!"

"Carmie!" Jenny squealed, as if she had never been so happy to see anybody in her life. "Get out here! It's Antarctica!"

"We've gotta go!" Carmie waved wildly. "Hurry! We're leaving!"

"What's up?" Jenny asked, shivering. "Where've you been?" She reached for her towel.

"Where's Jon?" Carmie asked.

"He had to go up to his house for something."

"Well, when is he coming back?"

"Don't ask me." Jenny pretended to laugh. "He's been gone for a year already. Why?"

"We have to go right now. It's my mom. Sorry. I'll tell you all about it. I have the most incredible thing to tell you. But do you want to leave Jon a message or something?"

"What for?" Jenny laughed. "I told him maybe I'd be here when he gets back, maybe I won't. He remembers where I live. In the B.H., right?" Jenny smiled at Carmie. "We are the girls from the B.H. Besides, it's okay if we go. This is getting boring."

Chapter 14

* * * * *

SUPERSTAR OF THE B.H.
By Carmie Hoffman

We hear moody rock music. The camera pans in to show CARMIE HOFFMAN's mansion in Malibu. Two Malibu girls walk up to the door and ring the doorbell. You can tell they are nervous. A butler, MAXWELL, opens the door.

MAXWELL

Good afternoon. Are you here for Miss Carmie?

The girls nod. Maxwell walks them down a long rich hallway and out into the backyard. Beautiful Carmie Hoffman is polishing her new surfboard in a back shed.

CARMIE

Hey! Didn't I see you guys at the beach once?

MALIBU GIRLS

Yeah. We hope you don't mind we found out where you live. We just had to meet you.

CARMIE

That's cool. You can't help it. Lots of times people just want to see where I live.

GIRLS

You're so lucky. You have the coolest mother and your own personal butler. How perfect is that?

CARMIE

Well, the only thing that can be really perfect is that one perfect wave out there.

GIRL NUMBER ONE

Wow. Do you ever see that one really cute surfer guy, Jon?

CARMIE

Oh, sure. I ride with him every now and then. He's cute. But my boyfriend is a real hottie.

GIRL NUMBER ONE

Do we know him? Is he famous?

GIRL NUMBER TWO

Can I carry your surfboard for you out to your car?

GIRL NUMBER ONE

No, can I?

"Carmie!" Carmie's mother called from the hallway. "Did you hear me?" Her voice already sounded weaker than it had the day before. "Do you want me to put your viola in the car? Where's the bow? You're going to be late!"

"That's okay," Carmie called back. "Don't worry about it." She closed her notebook and lifted Fluff Bucket off the end of her bed.

"Why don't you go for once?" she asked the cat. "See how you like it!"

Carmie went to her closet and pulled out a pair of jeans and a T-shirt. She looked in the mirror. She could still feel Coady's eyes smiling at her. Carmie smoothed her hair back with her hand and smiled. Somehow, they would be reunited.

"Let's go!" Carmie's mother called. "Rehearsal is today, sweetie, not tomorrow. I'm taking the viola out to the car."

Carmie looked in the mirror again. Coady could be waiting for her that day at the pier. But would he even remember her the next day? In the car, Carmie watched her mother fumble like an old lady to turn the ignition. Then her mother flicked through the radio stations to find people talking.

"Go into my wallet and get a dollar out of there in case you want a soda or something," Elaine said.

Carmie reached into her mother's bag and looked. "It's not in here."

"It's in there," Elaine said. "Look again."

"That's okay," Carmie said. She dropped the purse back on the floor. "If I need anything to drink, I'll just get dehydrated." She looked at her mother. Elaine held the wheel tightly and stared straight ahead at the road.

"Don't you just wish we were going back to the beach today to see your friends?" Carmie asked.

"This is rehearsal day," Carmie's mother said. "I don't wish it was any other day."

Carmie felt angry inside. How could her mother have forgotten the day before that quickly?

"One day you'll be glad you kept at this," Elaine said. "Believe me. Playing an instrument is good. You won't have to regret that you gave up something you were good at."

Carmie looked at her mother more carefully. Was this her way of saying she should never have given up surfing? Carmie wanted to scream at her that they should go back to the beach, but she knew it wouldn't do any good. Her mother would still turn back to normal. Didn't her mother understand that this was why she was so sick? She never should have quit surfing. Didn't she get that if she went back to Moondoggie that day, she could surf again? Was this what would happen to Carmie if she gave up surfing now?

"You have your cell phone in case you need me to pick you up, right?" Elaine asked, pulling up to the school.

"Yeah." Carmie got out of the car. She opened the back door and slid the viola case off the backseat, then folded down the handle and held it under her arm as if it was a surfboard.

"Don't worry," Carmie said. "I probably won't drop dead walking home in this disgusting heat."

"Play well," Elaine said.

"Hang loose," Carmie said.

"Right." Elaine laughed. Carmie saw her eyes twinkling. "Hang loose, sweetie."

* * *

"Let's take that from the fourth bar again, people," Mr. Adler called from the front of the room. Mr. Adler was the music teacher and also the orchestra conductor. He lifted his baton. Carmie looked at the clock.

"All eyes on me," Mr. Adler said, looking right at Carmie. "You have such potential. But how can you know when your part comes in if you don't watch me?"

Carmie felt her face flush. She didn't want to look at Mr. Adler. He was almost completely bald and he had a nose like a potato that somebody had sat on. Carmie wanted to save her eyes for Coady. She saw him in the water. She saw his gentle smile as she jumped into the ocean. She pulled her viola bow across the strings, slowly and evenly, as if it was a surfboard gliding over a baby wave. She saw Jon looking at her, and then Jenny thinking how lucky Carmie was to be with Coady. She saw her mother sitting on the shore, and she saw her mother's face. It was happy and alive and almost pretty, as it had looked when she was out on Jon's surfboard. Carmie almost saw Moondoggie's hand-some face smiling at her mother. Then she tried to see her father's face. It was hard to see, because he was all the way in Indiana. Suddenly Carmie felt a wave of guilt rush over her. Was she forgetting him?

"See you next week," Mr. Adler finally said. "Remember, we have our recital next month. I don't want Beethoven to roll over in his grave when he hears us play his sym-phony. And don't forget to practice. Practice your parts.

Practice does make perfect. That's the only thing that does it. Believe me."

*　*　*

Carmie started home. She passed Larry's Upholstery, with the stuffed owl on top of the building, and the Gonzales Market. Carmie had walked past that store a thousand times since she was a little girl, and the sign that said LECHE, CARNE Y DULCES in black letters.

"*Hola*, Carmie," Silvia called from the doorway. Silvia owned the store with her husband.

"*Hola*." Carmie waved with her viola case. Silvia laughed. It was eleven o'clock and it was already burning hot. Carmie thought of the ocean and the cool breeze dancing off the shore. She looked up. The sun here was not smiling at her. What did the sun have to smile about when it was stuck in the Valley?

Carmie fumbled to get her cell phone out of her back pocket. Then she punched in Jenny's number as fast as she could.

"One ringy-dingy. Two ringy-dingys." Carmie's heart started to race.

"Hey," she said when the message machine clicked on. "Where are you? Don't you know you're supposed to be there when I'm trying to call you? This is an emergency. Listen! We've got to get back to Malibu this afternoon. Only you can convince my mom to take us there. She'll listen to you! Trust me. You won't regret this. Call me on my cell. It's Jon."

Carmie closed her phone. She laughed at her own great sense of humor. Even though Jenny pretended that she didn't care about seeing Jon again, Carmie knew better. Then Carmie felt frightened. What if she needed to go back again after Jenny left on her family's vacation? Or what if her mother liked Moondoggie, but Moondoggie ended up having another girlfriend and that made her mom get even sicker? Wasn't that why she had gotten sick in the first place? Because Carmie's father had found his new girlfriend, Evelyn?

Carmie's cell rang.

"Surf's up, dudette," Carmie answered. "Are you over there yet?"

"Over where?" a man's voice said. Carmie stopped. "Is this Carmie? My firstborn honeybunch?"

"Hi, Daddy!" Carmie giggled. "Yes, it is me. I just thought that you would be my friend Jenny."

"Oh, sure. Jenny," Carmie's father said. "I remember Jenny. I was just hoping you hadn't forgotten me."

"I was going to call you." Carmie tried not to sound guilty.

"So, is Jenny's mom taking you to the beach?"

"Uh-huh," Carmie said. "I'm just walking home now from orchestra. It's like a thousand degrees outside."

"How's your mother?"

"I don't know," Carmie said.

"Is she still taking that one medicine?"

"I suppose," Carmie said.

"Well, listen, honeybunch. I just had a moment because I'm at work. Now, I don't want you to be afraid to use that

96

cell phone. That's why I got it for you. To call me!" Carmie's father laughed. "You know if you need me, I'm always here. And if it's an emergency and anything happens with your mom, you should call Aunt Raleigh."

"I know," Carmie said.

"You know I'm going to try to fly in for your orchestra recital at the very end of the summer."

"Oh, right," Carmie said. "Mommy told me. I'll call you a bunch of times before then." Carmie was glad the very end of the summer still seemed like a long time away. "And I swear I won't always answer the phone 'Surf's up'!"

"Okay," Carmie's father said, laughing. "I love you. If you are or if you aren't a surfer girl." Carmie wondered why he had said that. Did he secretly hope Carmie would be a surfer girl so that she wouldn't be so boring that her husband would leave her someday?

"I love you too, Daddy," Carmie said.

"Take good care of your mother, honeybunch."

"I will," Carmie said. "I promise."

Carmie hung up. She tried to pick up the pace. Now there was no doubt in her mind what she should do. She had to keep her promise to her father.

The cell rang again. Carmie opened the phone.

"Surf's up, dudette," she said, laughing. "Are you over there yet? Surf's definitely up!"

Chapter 15

"I wish," Jenny said too loudly on the phone. "Surf's definitely down. My mom's paranoid about me even going outside today because I got burned yesterday."

"Where?" Carmie panicked. "Just tell her you'll put on a lot of sunscreen. You don't even have to take your clothes off!"

"I tried that," Jenny said. "It's useless. She won't cave. She says I can go back tomorrow maybe if I'm all packed for the trip."

"Tomorrow?" Carmie asked. "I don't think my mom can go tomorrow!"

"If that guy really likes you, he'll still be there tomorrow." Jenny laughed.

"Who?" Carmie tried to act surprised. "You mean Coady? I don't really care so much about him. There're other reasons why we should go back today. Like the day after tomorrow you're leaving. Don't you want to see Jon?"

"He can wait!" Jenny laughed. "Besides, if he's not there

tomorrow, there will be a thousand other stupid guys out there going, 'Watch me! Watch me!' If Jon likes me, he could have called me."

"But does he even have your phone number?" Carmie asked.

"I don't know," Jenny said. "My mom said that if a guy wants to take you out on a date, he'll find some way to get your phone number."

Carmie sighed. She knew that whenever Jenny started a sentence with "My mom said," Jenny believed it was true. No matter what.

"My dad got five DVDs," Jenny said. "Good ones. Besides, it's too hot to do anything outside. Want to come over?"

"Yeah, I guess," Carmie said. Then she said goodbye and hung up. She tried to see Coady's eyes saying, "It's okay, darling. I can wait until tomorrow. I can wait for you forever if I have to." Jenny was right. If Coady really liked her, he could get her phone number.

Carmie opened the front door and shoved her viola case into the closet.

"I'm home!" she called. "Mommy! Anybody home?" Her voice turned angry. "Anybody dead?" she called. Fluff Bucket stretched on the sofa.

Carmie's mother came into the room. She looked tired and she was changing her clothes to go somewhere. Her voice sounded nervous.

"I've been calling you, but your line has been busy," Elaine said.

"Why?" Carmie asked. "What is it? What's wrong?"

"Remember this morning when you said you couldn't find my wallet in my purse? That was because I left it at the beach. Right on the blanket. I was showing everybody old pictures, and can you believe how stupid? I must have just left it there."

"How do you know it's there?" Carmie asked.

"Because they called me. There was just a message on the machine after I dropped you off. I guess it was Sean."

"You mean Moondoggie?" Carmie asked, trying not to laugh at his name.

"Well, I suppose Moondoggie if you want to call him that." Elaine gave Carmie a look. "That's what everybody called him when we were kids. Do you know where that nickname comes from? It's from the old beach movies with Gidget and her boyfriend, Moon—"

"But how did he even get our phone number?" Carmie interrupted. Her mind was racing.

"Well, it's right there in my wallet! With your baby pictures and my credit cards and the rest of my life. And it's already almost noon." Elaine looked at herself in the mirror.

"Do we have to go pick it up?" Carmie asked. She tried to keep her voice from sounding excited. Coady had found her number. He'd had his father slip the wallet out of the purse and then call because he was too shy to ask on his own.

"I'm hoping Aunt Raleigh's going to call me back," Elaine said. "I'm hoping she can drive me there and then I can just run down the beach and get it. But her cell isn't even on. I need to get down there and get back. I don't want to get stuck in Friday traffic. Frankly, I don't know if I'm not too tired to do all that driving today."

"I can go with you," Carmie said. "I'll make sure you stay awake. Besides, Aunt Raleigh probably won't be home until late."

"Well, you may be right," Elaine said. "I know you wanted to go to the beach today, but we're just running in and running out. I don't want you to be disappointed when we don't stay."

"It's okay," Carmie said. "I just need to change my clothes."

"I should probably have a cup of coffee first," Elaine said. "And I'm just going to finish getting dressed and that's it. Do you want to ask Jenny if she wants to come for the ride?"

"No, that's okay," Carmie said, starting down the hallway to her room. "She'll want to stay the whole day. And by the way, orchestra was really good today, Mom." Carmie opened her closet.

Coady had seen her in a towel the day before. This time she could get away with wearing jeans. That would be okay for someone just walking down the beach and back, looking for a wallet. Carmie took out her best faded black jeans and a pretty pink short top. She turned around in the mirror to see how her cell phone looked sticking out of her back pocket.

"I'll be starting the car," Elaine called. "Do you know what I did with my keys?"

Carmie gave her back pocket another look. She thought of Jenny. What was she going to say to Jenny? She took out her cell.

"One ringy-dingy . . . Two ringy-dingys . . . My mom needs me to go with her to run errands," Carmie said to Jenny's answering machine. "She's weird again. Keep your fingers crossed that I make it back alive." She tried to laugh. Then she felt bad. "I'll tell you all about it when I get home."

*　*　*

Carmie watched her mother drive. She saw that her mother had put light-green eyeshadow on the corners of her eyelids, where just before they had looked a little runny. Elaine was wearing pretty orange-pink lipstick. Carmie never saw her mother wearing makeup unless she had to go somewhere fancy with Aunt Raleigh and Uncle Roy, which only happened about once a year. Carmie liked the way her mother looked, even though she was still holding the steering wheel too tightly.

"You're okay, Mommy. Right?" Carmie asked.

"I'm fine," Elaine said softly.

"Mommy," Carmie asked, "did you used to go to Malibu all the time?"

"We used to come in the summer," Elaine said, blushing. "Aunt Raleigh and I. We came here to rebel."

"What do you mean?" Carmie asked. "You mean like you went to war?"

"Something like that," Elaine said, smiling. "But those were different times. That was the seventies. We rebelled

102

against everything. We just wanted to get away from Grandma and Grandpa. They wanted us to grow up to be like them. They wanted us to get good jobs and work at the post office like Grandma did. We didn't want to be square like a stamp." Elaine laughed. "We didn't want to be in the Valley and they didn't want us coming to Malibu, so that's why we came. Just to show them we could do what we wanted."

"You mean they didn't ever want to give you a ride?"

"And how!" Elaine said, checking her rearview mirror. "They didn't want us hanging out with those 'beach bums.' And in those days we didn't have our own car. Hardly any kids could afford their own cars. And we didn't know anybody who liked to go to the beach as much as we did. So Raleigh and I had to take four buses or else we just hitchhiked."

Carmie looked at her mother. She couldn't imagine her standing out on the road.

"Of course you'd have to be crazy to get into a car with a stranger today," Elaine said. "We were crazy then. But we were in love—l-u-v."

"You mean with a boyfriend?"

"With the ocean. With the whole thing. And I know you would never ever do that. Right?"

"What?" Carmie asked. "Have a boyfriend?"

"No," Elaine said. "Hitchhike."

"Right, Mom." Carmie laughed. "I'm out there hitching a ride every chance I can get. Especially to go to orchestra practice. I'd do anything to get to orchestra."

"That's good," Elaine said.

Carmie looked at her mother. Her mother had never told her this much about anything. Carmie couldn't stop asking questions. "But in the olden days, weren't you and Aunt Raleigh ever afraid you wouldn't fit in with all those kids?" Carmie asked.

"What do you mean?" Elaine said.

"I mean because you weren't from there. You know. Because you and Aunt Raleigh weren't real Malibu people. Because you lived in Sherman Oaks."

"Well, in the 'olden days,'" Elaine said, smiling, "when I was a girl, before they had electricity and cell phones and e-mail, Malibu was already starting to get crowded. But it still wasn't as packed as it is today. There were hardly any girls who knew how to surf. Like maybe three. People worshipped the surf. If you came to surf Malibu or you knew a local, you belonged."

Elaine turned right onto the Pacific Coast Highway. She rolled down her window and smiled. Carmie looked up at the sun smiling down on her. Her heart pounded. Couldn't her mother see? She definitely knew a local. Carmie was there to surf. She belonged.

Elaine made a slow left turn into the Malibu Beach parking lot.

"There's no place to park in here," Carmie said. "I can run down and get the wallet. It will just take me a minute." She tried to make her voice sound casual.

"I don't want you to get lost," Elaine said.

"I'm not going to get lost." Carmie laughed, opening the door. "Those people are in the same place as yesterday. Right?"

"I'm sure," Elaine said, as if she was thinking. "By the pier. They've probably been in the same place for twenty years."

"You just stay right here and rest from the drive, Mommy. I'll be right back."

"Okay. But be careful," Elaine said.

Carmie got out of the car.

"Thongs!" Elaine called. She handed Carmie her flip-flops. "You can burn up your feet out there."

Carmie smoothed her hair with her hand and headed down the beach. She put her hand in her back pocket, held in her stomach and tilted her face high into the sun as if she was letting it all just seep in. The ocean smelled cool. Its peaceful sounds filled up the beach even though there were hardly any waves breaking.

"This rocks," Carmie said softly, as if she didn't care that people on the beach could see she was talking to herself. They would know that, even though she was wearing long black jeans, she belonged. Carmie was the real thing. She was pure Malibu.

Carmie walked past all the towels with girls sunbathing on them, and the guys staring at the ocean, and then back at the girls. The girls' laughs were too soft, as if the girls knew they were being idolized. Carmie pretended to look straight ahead at the pier. Coady would look at her. He would look at her as if he was completely surprised she was there. His whole face would turn red. Suddenly a chill ran down Carmie's back. What if he didn't blush at all? Suddenly she wished Jenny was there, laughing too loudly. Carmie had been wrong. She didn't belong there.

Carmie saw somebody in a pink and lime bikini walking toward her. It was Barb from the day before, with her friend Eva.

"Hey!" Carmie tried to say in her most laid-back voice.

Barb looked at Carmie as if she was trying to remember where she had seen her. Then Barb nudged Eva's elbow.

"Hey," Barb said to Eva. "It's a Val."

Carmie could feel them laughing behind her. How did she know that Barb and Coady weren't walking up and down the beach at that very moment looking for each other?

"Carmie!" She thought she heard someone calling. She kept walking. "Carmie!" the voice called again. Carmie stopped and looked behind her. Her mother was waving and running up the beach. Her long legs peeked out of her sarong. Carmie had never been so glad to see her mother in her life, even though she had never seemed less like her mother in her life. Everything was changing so fast. Was this finally the mother Carmie had always wanted?

"I found a space." Elaine laughed, catching her breath. "Just after I dropped you off. How lucky is that?"

"It's good." Carmie still tried to sound as if she was laid-back. She reached for her mother's hand. She didn't want anybody to see she was holding it, but she didn't want to let go, either.

"No, you're supposed to say, 'It's great!' " Elaine laughed. "At Malibu you say everything is great. Surf's up. Great. Got a cold? Great. Get your wallet back, you say 'Great.' "

"But what if something is bad, Mommy?" Carmie laughed.

"There's only one thing that's not great." Elaine laughed. "If the ocean is totally flat. Then you say 'Bummer.' "

"Nobody says that anymore." Carmie laughed.

"You're probably right." Elaine laughed.

They walked past the pier. Carmie could see the blanket ahead. She could see Moondoggie. Then she could see Coady. He was sitting in the sand, looking at the water.

"Great," Carmie said out loud to herself. "This is going to be so Great."

Chapter 16

"Hey!" Moondoggie got up off the blanket. "Afternoon, ladies." He smiled at Elaine. "Hey, Carmie." He patted her on the head. "Howzit?"

"You know"—Carmie stumbled, trying not to look at Coady—"it's great!" Coady looked straight out at the water.

"Hey!" Aloha Fats raised his baby high over his shoulders to say hello. "You came back!"

"She forgot her wallet, man," Moondoggie said, laughing.

"That's a drag," Cotton Candy said.

"That's how she planned it," Moondoggie said, smiling. "Just a scam to get back down here where she belongs."

"Right, Moondoggie." Elaine laughed. "You're still on the case." Moondoggie reached for Elaine's hand, and Elaine sat down on the blanket as if she was settling in. Coady was looking straight ahead and ignoring Carmie. Carmie felt sick. Why was her mother sitting when she'd promised they would just get her wallet and get out of there?

Elaine held out her hand. "Slide the wallet right there," she said to Moondoggie. "I hope the five hundred dollars that I had in there is still there."

"Hey!" Moondoggie laughed, moving closer to Elaine. "Even if it isn't, it won't be a loss," he said, winking. "I promise. Right, dude?" he asked Coady.

"Uh-huh," Coady said. He stared ahead. Then he turned and looked at Carmie.

"Hey," he said.

"Hey," Carmie said back. Without his glasses, Coady looked even cuter than the day before. Carmie's heart pounded. Had he been ignoring her before just because he was embarrassed? Could everyone see what an idiot Carmie was, just standing there, liking him?

"Only one second, sweetie," Elaine said to Carmie.

Carmie looked at Coady. Suddenly something awful hit her. Coady didn't know anything at all about the wallet. It was only Moondoggie who had dug for her and her mom's number.

"Come on, Carmie." Moondoggie reached for her hand. "Cool your dogs for a while."

"Cool," Carmie said, as if she knew exactly what he was talking about.

"I miss you guys," Elaine said, closing her wallet. Carmie had never once heard her mother say she missed Carmie's father. She hardly ever heard her say she missed Grandma, and Grandma was dead. Carmie felt afraid. Was her mother okay? Did she even know what she was talking about? If she missed these guys so much, how come she had never told Carmie about them? Couldn't she see she was making a fool of herself? Carmie glanced at Coady again. She never wanted to miss him. She just wanted to get herself and her mother out of there.

"The traffic, Mom," Carmie said. "Remember?"

"You just got here," Cotton Candy said. "Hey." She reached into her cooler. "You want a smoothie?"

"No, thanks," Carmie said. "We've got to go. Remember, Mom? It's Friday."

"So stay the weekend," Moondoggie said, laughing. "Candy, there've got to be a couple of spare suits around here, right? These ladies didn't come prepared."

"Dig it," Cotton Candy said. "I've even got a couple of old O'Neills up at my place you can put on."

Carmie could feel the hairs standing up on her back. She didn't want to be stuck all weekend sleeping on the beach with a bunch of homeless people and having Coady not remember the day before. She didn't want to wear somebody's old O'Neill. What was an O'Neill, anyway?

"Thanks," Elaine said, taking the smoothie from Candy. "But after I finish this," she said, "we're out of here."

Carmie looked at the smoothie. She felt relieved that it wasn't the big size. Then she looked at Coady. If he was going to change, he was going to have to do it fast.

"Yo, brah!" a guy called, coming up the beach. Carmie turned and saw four surfer guys with white-blond hair. Her heart stopped.

"Hey, dude," Coady called back to the first guy. "Whassup?"

"It's Lake Atlantic out there, brah," the second guy said.

"Tell me about it," Coady said, laughing. "Bummer." He

looked at Carmie. Then he smiled. Carmie tried not to look back. Was he saying she was the bummer? She could feel the other guys turning to look at her. She patted her back pocket and her cell. Then the surfers looked away like they knew she was nobody.

"Hey," one of the other guys said, walking up to a surfboard standing in the sand. "Dude!" He stopped. "It's a longboard. Look at that thing! How old is that thing, dude?"

"That's like from the dinosaur era," Aloha said with a laugh.

"It's an original Dewey Weber, man." Moondoggie stood up to show it.

"Who's Dewey Weber?" the surfer asked.

"Do your homework, son," Moondoggie said, looking at him. "How are you gonna be a decent surfer if you don't have some reverence for your surf history?" The surfer looked at Moondoggie. Then he looked at everyone else on the blanket as if he was trying to figure out whether they were old enough to be history.

"Hey, man," the second guy said to the third guy, "don't be a total brain freeze." He turned to Moondoggie. "You're Sean Woodward. Right, man?"

"I'm afraid so," Moondoggie said, laughing.

"Cool!" the second guy said. "You were, like, world champion three times, right?"

"Yeah, I was. In my day." Moondoggie tried to laugh. "And this is Aloha Fats." He pointed at Aloha. "You know anything about him?"

"I got fat." Aloha laughed, patting his stomach. "That's all they need to know."

"Right," Moondoggie said. "And that he only won Pipeline Masters twice."

"Candy 'the Cotton Candy Rip Curler' Carlin," Candy said, waving her hand high. "Don't forget the chicks. We were out there, man. We were the first. I got some prize money. I hyped a couple of T-shirts." She laughed.

With their mouths open, the surfer boys looked at everybody.

"And this is Elaine Koven," Moondoggie said. Carmie looked at her mother. What could Moondoggie say? Had her mother once been somebody?

"Elaine Hoffman now." Elaine laughed. "Well, I'm still Elaine Hoffman but I'm not married to a Hoffman anymore. But I'm still nobody. My sister, Raleigh, used to surf here too. She was better than me, really. I never got a nickname out here. Believe me. I'm nobody. I didn't win anything."

"But you could have," Moondoggie said. His voice sounded serious. He looked at her. Elaine looked away.

"And I'm 'nobody''s daughter." Carmie laughed. She didn't know what else to say.

"Yes, this is my first prize." Elaine patted Carmie gently on the back. "I got out there the other day for the first time in years. That's about it for me."

"Hey, dude," the second surfer said to Coady, "what are you doing all the way down here?"

"I told you he hangs with Sean," the first surfer said. "Coady Woodward. And that's Sean Woodward."

Carmie looked at Coady. She liked the way "he hangs with Sean" sounded. Everything about Coady's life with

112

his dad had to be so much easier than Carmie's with her mother or father. Coady looked at the water. Then he looked at Carmie, and Carmie's heart pounded. His eyes were focused on her. They were saying, "You and me. We just hang. We belong together."

"Hey, dude," the first surfer said, "we're going back up the other end of the beach. All the frosted chicks are up there. So?"

Carmie cringed. Were they looking at her as if they knew she was a dog?

"I'm good here," Coady said. He gave the first surfer a high five.

"Later," the first surfer said.

"Later. Nice to meet you," the second said to everyone on the blanket.

"Later." The third surfer nodded to Carmie.

"Great," Carmie said, looking down. She didn't want anybody to see her smiling.

"Well, hey!" Elaine said, putting down her smoothie. "Thanks for this. And my wallet. It's getting late. Ready, sweetie?"

"No, wait!" Coady stood up in the sand. "Look." He laughed, pointing at the ocean. "Looks like there's at least a couple of two-footers coming in."

"Righteous," Moondoggie said, laughing. "Come on, Elaine. Tie up your skirt. Let's go for it."

"I'm going for the freeway," Elaine said, giggling. "Maybe another time."

"When?" Moondoggie asked. "What other time? This is it!"

Coady pulled his surfboard out of the sand. He looked at Carmie, his eyes saying, "Don't you know my dad is right? You've got what it takes to be a good surfer."

"You don't have your suit on underneath that?" he asked.

"I didn't know I was staying here this long," Carmie said. She looked at the ocean. It was clear and flat and royal blue. In the distance she could see baby waves rolling in like escalators. This was her last chance.

"I'm sorry."

"No worries," Coady said. He hardly looked at her. Then he started toward the water.

"I guess a baby wave is better than nothing," Cotton Candy said, standing up. She pulled out a bar of wax and started rubbing the wax onto her board.

Carmie gazed at her mother with Moondoggie. His eyes twinkled at the corners like Coady's. They looked cool and almost handsome, the way they must have looked when he was still young. Elaine was laughing. She seemed wide awake and healthy. Carmie turned to watch Coady walk. The tops of his shoulders were peeling from the sun. The red and black stripes on his surf trunks seemed to wave gently in the wind.

"Are you okay, Mommy?" Carmie asked, turning.

"Of course," Elaine said. "Don't worry. Ready?"

Carmie looked at the water again. She rolled up the bottoms of her jeans.

"Wait!" she called out as loudly as she could. "Coady. Dude." Then she ran as hard as she could.

"Carmie!" she could hear her mother calling behind her. "What are you doing?"

"All right!" She could hear Cotton Candy and Moondoggie whooping it up. Then they got fainter and fainter. The ocean got closer and bluer. Coady stopped and waited for Carmie to catch up.

"All right," Coady said, smiling. "You sure?"

"Uh-huh," Carmie said, trying to catch her breath. "Just for a few minutes, so my mother doesn't freak." She rolled her jeans higher. Then she followed Coady to the shore.

"Let's roll!" Carmie cheered. She ran into the water.

"Hurry!" Coady called back to her.

"Ice!" Carmie froze. She was too far from the blanket to turn back and too far from Coady to keep going. The water was already well past the cuffs of her jeans. She stood there. Her body was in too much shock to feel anything other than her sopping underpants sucking up her skin like a thousand iced leeches.

"Dunk under," Coady called. "Remember?" Then he disappeared into the water to show her. He popped back up. His beautiful hair flattened on his head. "See? Then you don't feel it anymore."

Carmie tried to cry, "I can't!" But it wouldn't come out. Then she dunked. She could hear her heartbeat under the water. She shot back up. "Ice!" She laughed. "Ice!"

Coady looked out at the water. "Don't be afraid. It's a two-footer!" he called. "This is going to be perfect for you. Want to?"

The ocean floor gently lifted Carmie up and set her

down until finally there was no floor to walk on below her. She could see Coady's face. Her thick hair was completely matted back. Her pink top was pressed against her breasts like in a sexy movie, but Carmie didn't think Coady could see anything. The light padding of her bra was bobbing up and down in her shirt as if it had nowhere else to go. Coady held the board steady with his hand.

"All you have to do is just paddle a little like yesterday. Right?"

"Uh-huh," Carmie said, trying to get onto the board on her stomach.

"I'll hold it," Coady said. "I've got my eye on the wave. You look behind you. Just over your shoulder like that." He glanced behind him to demonstrate. "Then, when you feel that wave coming—that's yours."

"Uh-huh," Carmie said. She glanced behind her. She caught Coady's eye. She felt completely ridiculous and somehow safe.

"Okay, now paddle," Coady said. "Come on. Paddle hard. Just a few strokes."

Carmie paddled as hard as she could. She felt the wave coming behind her, pushing her.

"Okay, now just hold on to the board!" Coady cried out. "Here you go. Go for it!"

"Whoaaaa!" Carmie squealed. She was flying. She could see the white water ahead of her and the shore rushing up to meet her. She could see the blanket and what had to be her mother jumping off it.

"This one is mine." Carmie hummed to herself. The shore was getting too close now. She didn't want to go

116

home. She didn't want to see her mother turn back into her mother again. But she could hardly wait to tell Jenny all about this. Should she? She didn't want to make Jenny jealous, but only Jenny could convince Elaine that they should go back to the beach the next day. And the next day was the last chance. Sunday Jenny was leaving. Monday Elaine had to go back to work. The next day everything had to change forever.

Chapter 17

Carmie got underneath all her covers. She could hear her jeans and pink top and underwear in the kitchen, being tossed from side to side in the dryer. Her legs and feet still felt cold, even though it was hot in the Valley. She was making a list of everything she had to do to make sure the next day turned out just right. Then her cell phone rang.

"Carmie's surf report," Carmie answered, laughing. "So you know exactly what you're going to say to my mom tomorrow morning, right?"

"Well, not exactly," a voice said.

"Oh, hi, Aunt Raleigh." Carmie laughed again. "Sorry. I thought you were somebody else."

"I thought I was somebody else too," Aunt Raleigh said, laughing. "But now, much to my surprise, I find out I'm me!"

"Me too."

"That's good." Aunt Raleigh laughed again. "I wouldn't want you to be anybody else. I had to call you on your cell because I tried to call for hours," Aunt Raleigh said.

"Nobody answered and I guess you didn't have your machine on. So somebody who wanted to call your mom called me. Is your mom still up?"

"She's asleep," Carmie said. "She did a lot of driving today."

"Oh, really?" Aunt Raleigh asked. "Where to?"

"We had to drive back to Malibu Beach because Mom forgot her wallet."

"Oh," Aunt Raleigh said. Her voice sounded different.

"Yeah," Carmie said. "Well, I think Mom tried to call you first," she added. Why did Aunt Raleigh sound this way?

"Ask her please to call me tomorrow morning when she wakes up," Aunt Raleigh said. "Okay?"

"Okay," Carmie said.

"You'll remember, doll?" Aunt Raleigh asked. "Because it's important."

"I will," Carmie said. She hung up. What if whatever was important was supposed to happen tomorrow? It couldn't.

Fluff Bucket walked into Carmie's room and jumped onto her bed. She sat on Carmie's legs and curled up for a nice nap. Carmie reached to her nightstand for her famous movie script notebook.

FAMOUS MALIBU BEACH MOVIE
By C. Hoffman

NEXT SCENE:
Inside the beach mansion. CARMIE HOFFMAN, wearing a perfect pair of white shorts and a white bathing suit top (that doesn't need

padding), is carrying her third surfboard to her car. A woman Carmie's mother's age, only it's not Carmie's mother, comes into the room. It is Carmie's aunt BRITNEY.

AUNT BRITNEY
Let me remind you, you and your mother aren't driving anywhere. She's not telling you the truth. The awful truth. You want to know what the ocean does to you? Look at me. Look at this cane.

Just then, CARMIE'S MOTHER comes into the room, raising her arm to Aunt Britney. She looks almost pretty and she's dressed in white.

CARMIE'S MOM
(screams) Britney, stop it. You're not well! You need to see a doctor. You don't know what you're talking about.

Aunt Britney drops her cane. They wrestle each other to the floor.

Carmie opened one eye. Her notebook and pen had been thrown across the floor. Fluff Bucket was asleep on her face. She heard her mother talking to someone in the kitchen. Carmie's heart started beating fast. It was Jenny.

"I'm going to wake her sleeping butt up right now." Jenny laughed. "We're so lucky you'll take us again. Because this is like the last day of summer for me. You know in Colorado they don't have an ocean."

Carmie sat on the edge of her bed, cringing. She never told Jenny to say Colorado didn't have an ocean.

"Carmie said you even saw people you used to know who

120

live there. You're so lucky. My mom and dad always say they wish we had enough money to buy a house at the beach."

"Well, I wish I had enough money to buy a house at the beach too," Elaine said. Her voice sounded soft and dreamy. Carmie smiled. Nobody could resist Jenny. Jenny was a genius.

"I'm awake!" Carmie ran into the kitchen. "Thank you, Mommy." She threw her arms around her mother. "You're sure you're okay to drive us, right?"

"As long as we don't stay too long," Elaine said. "I have things I have to do before I go back to work Monday and it's an awful lot of driving."

"Well, I have an idea," Jenny said. Her voice sounded too excited. "If it's too much driving, maybe Carmie's aunt Raleigh can come too. She knows how to drive, right? Then you can share. That's what my mom and dad always do on long trips."

"No, let's just go," Carmie said quickly. "Besides, I forgot, Mommy. Aunt Raleigh called. But she said not to call her back until later today. She had to do something important."

Carmie started down the hallway, her heart pounding. She could see Coady's eyes. How he had looked at her the day before when she'd come out of the water soaked and fearless. She had to tell this lie. She would tell Aunt Raleigh later she was sorry, she'd just forgotten the message.

"Come with me," Carmie said.

"I'm with you." Jenny pretended to march behind Carmie to her room.

"Your jeans are in the dryer," Carmie's mother called. "Let's get a move on!"

"This Coady guy better appreciate this," Jenny said, following Carmie into the bathroom. Carmie took her bathing suit top out of the hamper. She slid it on as fast as she could.

"I'm with you." Carmie laughed. "Who knows where Coady is even going to be? He's definitely a water boy."

"So is Jon." Jenny laughed. "He's a water baby boy."

Carmie reached for her other jeans. Then she took out a pair of blue jean shorts.

"I could never wear these," she said.

"Why not?" Jenny asked, as if she didn't know what Carmie was talking about. "You surfed in all your clothes yesterday! Shorts are all I'm wearing. We can be twins!"

"Girls!" Elaine called. "It's now or never."

Carmie pulled her white terry cover-up off the hanger. It wasn't good, but it wasn't 100 percent ugly, either. She stuffed her cell phone into the bottom of her sock drawer. Then she stroked the cat's belly. "Guard the house, Fluff Bucket," she said. She ran into the kitchen with Fluff Bucket behind her. She grabbed two pieces of tasteless, healthy spelt bread from the counter. "Watch TV if you want, Fluff. Make some popcorn. You may not be living here forever."

Chapter 18

"And if you're heading down to Malibu," the voice on the radio said, "you are heading into a gorgeous day. That is, if everybody hasn't beaten you to it. There's a body jam on the sand!"

"What else could there possibly be?" Elaine said. She rolled down her window and smiled at the ocean, putting her foot on the brake again.

"Body jam." Jenny squeezed Carmie into the corner. "This is worse traffic than at the mall," she said with a laugh. "Oh my God, did you see that? That guy was taking off his trunks right behind his car door. Wicked! I saw everything! Are you okay up there, Elaine?"

"I'm going to throw up back here," Carmie said. "I'm getting carsick." Carmie thought maybe coming back with Jenny was not such a good idea after all. "We're never going to find a place to park, Mom."

Elaine turned on her signal. She pulled right into the only open parking space on the Pacific Coast Highway.

"Good job, Mom," Carmie said proudly, throwing open the door.

"You'll be sure to bring your cell, Carmie, will you?" Elaine asked. "I need to call Aunt Raleigh. I haven't talked to her in two days. You remember her cell number, don't you?"

"I just realized I forgot it," Carmie said, feeling all around the backseat. "I don't even have my cell phone. Oh, great. I can't believe this."

"Me neither." Jenny laughed. "This is the first time in American history that that ever happened." She gave Carmie a look as if she knew something was up.

Carmie tried not to look back. She hoped she wasn't going to regret bringing Jenny along.

"Look at all those millions of black things in the water," Jenny said loudly.

"Wet suits." Elaine laughed. "And those are surfers in them. The water must be really cold."

"Wow!" Jenny laughed. "There's so many of them. You could never find somebody out there if you were looking for him."

Carmie cringed. Nothing seemed right that day. There were too many people. It didn't even seem like Malibu Beach. She should have just worn her blue jeans. Today she looked like everybody else who was wearing a regular white cover-up instead of a bikini. What would happen if Coady got one look at Jenny? Then Carmie saw Coady's face as it had looked when she was leaving the day before. His eyes had been telling her, "You so rock! Look at you! You're, like, fearless. I've never met a girl like you before."

124

Carmie smiled. Somewhere out there Coady was on his board waiting for her. All Carmie had to do was let Jenny look for Jon and head for the pier by herself.

"Here's a spot," Elaine called out.

"Right here?" Carmie asked. It looked like a spot, all right. A spot big enough for Fluff Bucket. "But don't you want to go down over by—"

"You're going to see the best surf breaking on this beach right here," Elaine said, opening the blanket. She sat down and looked straight ahead. "We've got a head-on view," she said dreamily, as if she was remembering something.

Carmie looked at the ocean. The waves were puffy and beautiful, like clouds rolling on top of the water.

"Are you going out there again today, Elaine?" Jenny asked. "I want to watch!"

"Who, me?" Elaine giggled. "Not with all those guys dropping in on each other and tearing the waves apart. There're way too many surf rats out there."

"Surf rats," Jenny repeated with delight. "Come on, Carmie," she said, taking off her T-shirt. "I smell a rat! Want to go look?"

Carmie looked at her mother. "Are you going to be okay here, Mommy?" she asked. There wasn't enough room that day for Elaine to open her sun umbrella. She looked so out of place and alone. "Wouldn't you rather be over there with your friends?" Carmie asked.

"I'll be fine, sweetie," Elaine said. "You don't have to worry about me."

"Well then, I'm going to watch Carmie surf," Jenny said. "I can't wait!"

"I don't think going out there alone is such a good idea, Carmie," Elaine said. "That water's cold and all those boards flying around can be dangerous. Believe me. Those waves are bigger than they look."

"I know." Carmie smiled as if her mother didn't know who she was talking to. "No worries."

Then she followed Jenny. Carmie watched everybody watching Jenny as they passed.

"So which one is Coady?" Jenny asked.

"I can't say I know," Carmie said. "It's hard to tell because they're all wearing O'Neills."

"What's that?" Jenny looked at Carmie.

"It's a kind of wet suit. It's, like, the best brand."

"Of course, my little surfologist." Jenny laughed.

Carmie felt her shoulders tense. Then she giggled. "Just call me Professor Surf."

"Yes, Professor Surf O'Neill." Jenny pretended to bow.

"It is so cool when you're out there," Carmie said, looking at the ocean. "When you're paddling and you can see that big wave coming behind you."

"Earth to Malibu Carmie," Jenny said. "Remember who you're talking to? It's me! Remember me?" Jenny jumped up and down, laughing. "So are you going to go out there or what?"

"Are you kidding?" Carmie laughed. "I'm not afraid of the waves. But that water's like ice! Maybe if I had a wet suit."

"I'd go out there," Jenny said. She ran far enough into the water to get her ankles wet. "Yeooow!" she squealed, running back to Carmie.

"Professor Surf." Jenny laughed. "Go out there with me. Don't you want to find Coady?"

Carmie made a shield with her hand as if she was trying to get a good look out at the water.

"Uh-oh," Jenny said. "That's him. That's got to be him."

"Who?" Carmie tried to look.

"Jon!" Jenny turned her back. "Don't look. Let's get out of here. I don't want him to see me."

Carmie looked. One wave after another was coming in from the back of the ocean like an up escalator. A tall guy with blondish hair was leading the way down the first wave. A hundred other guys were trying to stand up on the same ride. They fell off and toppled into each other. A boy with white, white hair was still standing. Carmie could tell he was Jon.

Another guy in the front lost his balance and went flying off his board like in a cartoon. Carmie laughed. Then she saw something that made her heart stop. It was glasses on a surfboard. Coady was wearing his glasses in the water.

Carmie watched him. His perfect lean body shifted its weight from side to side. His feet took tiny scampering steps up and then back down the board. Then he was one of the only guys still standing. Carmie was the only girl right there in a white cover-up. Wouldn't he see her? At any moment. Their eyes would meet. If only for a second. And he would smile.

"Hey, geek!" Carmie heard a guy calling over the sound of the breaking waves. Another guy jumped off the board beside him. Their arms were swinging as if they were going to slug each other.

"Locals only, dude!" another guy hollered. "You don't live here, you don't surf here."

Carmie tried to keep her eyes on Coady. What was he doing out there? Why did he have to be with people like Jon in the ocean that was his very life? Coady fell off his board. Carmie watched his head bob back out of the water as it had the first day he'd shown her how to warm up. She thought she saw him looking at her. His eyes were saying, "I am not like the rest of these fools."

"I think that was him," Carmie said to Jenny.

"Where?" Jenny jumped up and down even higher, like a cheerleader. Carmie could tell that Jon saw Jenny. She saw him smile at her. Jon turned his board around and leaped onto it as if he was a dolphin at Sea World. It was as if Carmie could hear him saying, "Watch me. Watch me."

"Those guys look so hilarious," Jenny squealed, pretending she didn't even notice Jon. "Those girls are so awesome. We should be out there!"

"Yeah, right." Carmie laughed. "That stuff might look easy. It's a lot harder than it looks."

"Come on, Professor." Jenny laughed. She unzipped her shorts and let them fall to her ankles. "If Jon can do it . . ."

Carmie looked at Jenny, then at the ocean. She didn't know what was coming over her, but the next thing she knew, she was running toward the water.

"Your cover-up!" she heard Jenny calling behind her. "You nut! You don't want to swim in that thing, do you?"

Carmie watched the green and blue flower on the pocket bob up and down as she ran. Then the water crashed into the pocket. The water was too cold. Too cold to stop.

Carmie dropped into it and then shot back up. She couldn't tell if she was laughing or crying. Her breathing just sounded loud. Now her hair was so matted against her face, she couldn't see.

"Girls rule!" she heard Jenny cheering as loudly as she could from the beach.

Carmie parted her hair away from her eyes with her hands as if she was cutting away a jungle of seaweed. Below her, she could already feel the baby tail ends of the big waves lifting her up higher than she had ever gone without Coady and setting her down on the ocean floor. She knew she couldn't go any farther.

"Hey!" some guy chasing his board called to Carmie. "This is a surfers-only beach. You could get diced out here by somebody's board, dude. Stop that one for me, will you?" The surfer pointed to a neon-bright board running away toward the whitewater.

"Sure!" Carmie moved as fast as she could to try to catch it. She thought if she could just reach it, she could somehow get on it on her stomach and be pushed back to the sand. Coady would finally see her, come out of the waves, tuck his surfboard under his arm and run to the shore.

Carmie took another step, and suddenly there was no floor beneath her. She bobbed up as high in the water as she could. She reached with all her might and touched the tail of the board. It was so much longer and heavier than the board she had been on with Coady.

"Girl in the white dress." A lifeguard's voice came over a megaphone. "Girl in the white dress. You're too far out. This is a surfing beach."

"I know," Carmie tried to call back. Her heart was pounding. She tried to see if any of the surfers were watching her. She used all her strength to steady the surfboard and hold on tight. She could see that the flying surfboards would crash down on her if she went out very much farther.

She flopped herself onto the board on her stomach as far up as she could, just waiting for it to take her close enough in for her to touch the ocean floor. "Whoa!" The surfer boy walked toward her. "Dude! That's good," he called.

Carmie pretended not to be able to stop the board until she thought for sure her feet could touch the ocean floor. Then she rolled off and held on to it. "Sorry," Carmie called, breathing deeply. The boy walked toward her, picked up his neon board with both hands and lifted it high over his head. Then he dropped it on the water and started paddling back out.

"Thanks, man," he called.

"It's cool." Carmie tried to sound relaxed.

"Come out of the water, please," the lifeguard called. Carmie worried about what would happen if she did. Would her mother be there? Would Jenny be laughing with everybody watching her? Was everybody just waiting to see what the only person on earth to wear a dress in the ocean looked like?

Carmie could hear the whoops of the surfers going for it. She remembered what it felt like to make that sound herself. Now she never wanted to look at another wave.

"Hey!" she heard a voice call from behind her. "Hey! I

know you!" The boy's voice laughed. "Wait up. Aren't you that Valley girl? You're Jenny's sidekick. Right?"

Carmie looked back. Jon was walking through the water toward her. His dimples and chest were glistening in the sun. Carmie pretended she couldn't hear him.

"Hey!" Jon called out again. "I forgot your name."

"Carmie!" she called. "I'm Carmie," she said, looking back.

"Yeah, right. Carmie. So, Carmie, where's your buddy?" Jon pretended to laugh.

"She's here." Carmie nodded toward the beach. Her arm was so cold she could hardly feel it. The sun was smiling down on her, but not hard enough. "Can't you hear her up there?"

"She didn't have what it takes to come out here," Jon said, laughing. "That's awesome."

"I guess." Carmie tried to smile. She wasn't awesome. She was frozen. She was an idiot who'd just made an incredible fool of herself in front of every guy in the ocean.

The beach looked closer and closer. Finally Carmie could see Jenny waving on the shore.

"Carmie Hoffman rocks," she called out too loudly, pretending she didn't see that Jon was right behind Carmie. "You go, girl!" Jenny cheered. She gave Carmie a high five.

"Jon's here," Carmie said, pointing.

"Where?" Jenny laughed.

Carmie sat down on the sand. She felt sick. She glanced at the ocean to see if anyone was looking. Then she pulled the white cover-up over her head as fast as she could. She had never been so cold in her life. She didn't even have a towel to wrap herself in.

A lifeguard walked toward her with his megaphone. Carmie looked up. She could feel her teeth chattering. He smiled. Then he squatted down to talk to Carmie.

"You okay?" He looked Carmie straight in the eye. It was him. It was the same lifeguard.

"Yes," Carmie said. "I'm sorry. I don't usually get into this much trouble. Honest."

"Yes, she does, Mr. Lifeguard Person." Jenny laughed. "But she doesn't mean to."

"You might want to go find a dry towel, surfer girl," the lifeguard said to Carmie. "And your mother." He looked Jenny up and down as if he liked what he saw. Then he started back toward his tower.

Jon came out of the water and shook his wet head on Jenny.

"No!" Jenny squealed with delight. "What are you doing here?"

"What you know I do here every day. What are you doing here?" He gave Jenny a long, slow smile.

"I'm just looking at all the cute boys." Jenny laughed. "But unfortunately for you, this is my last day here. I'm going to Colorado tomorrow."

"Oh yeah?" Jon said, moving in closer. "Aren't you afraid you're going to miss me?"

"Maybe," Jenny said in a long, slow, nauseating way.

"That's cool," Carmie said, standing up. She didn't care

anymore what anybody thought when they saw her. She had to move. "I'm going back. I've got to get a towel."

"No, wait!" Jenny said, putting her hand out to Jon. "One last sec, Carm."

"So are you moving to Colorado?" Jon asked Jenny.

"No." Jenny laughed. "I'm just going for two weeks."

"Oh, dude," Jon said, looking at the water. "I'm missing this set. Look at that! Watch me!" he called, running back out. "Don't go away. I mean it. Watch me!"

Jenny stood at the shore. Jon turned to look at her. She waved. She watched him run into the water until he was far out enough to drop his board and paddle. Then she ran after Carmie.

Chapter 19

"Can you believe that guy?" Jenny asked.

"I told you he liked you," Carmie said, moving fast.

"Well, of course he likes me." Jenny laughed. "What a burnout! Let's see if he asks for my number this time. Whatever. Are you okay? Don't you want to go back and wait for Coady?"

"He's probably way farther out than Jon was," Carmie said. "Those guys never come in when there's surf. I think he's, like, a professional surfer."

"Whoa," Jenny said.

"All I want now is my towel." She passed the Malibu girls lying on their perfect beach blankets. She could tell they were seeing her as the wet dog she knew she was. But at least she was the one who had gone in the water. Jenny hadn't even gone out there.

"I think I'll give him my number in Colorado," Jenny said, running to keep up. "You think I should? That will be the real test. My mother says if a boy really likes you,

134

he'll be happy to spend some money on you. And this is nothing."

Carmie was cold, and for the first moment in her life, she hated Jenny. She hated it when Jenny talked about all the things boys were supposed to do for her, as if she was a movie star. It was better that Coady hadn't come out. He would hate Jenny too.

Carmie got to the postage stamp–sized spot where their towels were. She dropped the sopping-wet cover-up on the sand and picked up her towel. Her mother wasn't there, but Carmie wasn't worried this time. It felt so good to be warm and safe that Carmie was afraid she would start to cry.

"Uh-oh," Jenny said. She shielded her eyes, like she was looking out at the ocean. "Oh my god, if she's out there, I want to watch again." Jenny laughed. "You know she's, like, a million times better than Jon!" Jenny turned as if she was going to run back to the shore. "I watched Mamma surf and today I watched her little baby, Carmie, surf!" Jenny said too loudly. "How come you're not freaking about your mother for the first time in your life?"

"Because," Carmie said. She wrapped the warm towel tightly around herself. "Follow me."

"Where?" Jenny asked, looking back.

"I've got to tell you something," Carmie said, standing up and heading toward the pier. The beach was so crowded it was hard to see if the big blanket was at the other side.

"What?" Jenny sounded excited. "Where are we going? Are there boys?"

"Well, sort of." Carmie laughed. "Maybe something even a little better than boys."

"What?" Jenny asked, running. "More boys?"

"What I've got to tell you is a secret. But I mean a real secret," Carmie said, stopping. Her brain was moving as fast as it could. She had to figure out a way to let Jenny know that she wasn't the only one who was God's gift to sand. She had to figure out a way to let Jenny see where her mom was, tell Jenny the secret and then get her out of there fast, in case Coady came back and saw Jenny. Carmie knew she was being immature, but it made her feel important, and she didn't hate Jenny anymore. It had to be good. But what was the secret?

"This better be really good." Jenny laughed. She was having a hard time keeping up with Carmie in the sand.

Carmie looked ahead. She could see the pier and the last lifeguard stand. Even with the crowd, she could see the surfboard that was too long and high standing up in the sand like a special fence that guarded the home of the legends. Carmie thought she saw Moondoggie. Her mother had to be close by.

"Where I'm taking you"—Carmie stopped, turned and looked Jenny square in the eye—"is a special place, even though it may seem kind of weird. These are all my mother's friends. From a long time ago."

"Your mom's friends?" Jenny asked. "I thought you said your mom didn't have any friends." She sounded nervous. "So what are they doing here?"

"They've never left here," Carmie said.

"Well, if this is so cool that it's a big secret," Jenny said, excited, "I won't want to leave here either."

Carmie panicked. "Yeah, but the point is you can only see them fast. They don't like strangers looking at them for more than a few minutes. Besides, you want to see this quick and get back to Jon before he leaves, don't you?"

Jenny looked at Carmie as if she was trying to figure out what Carmie was talking about. "I think I see your mom," Jenny said. "Who are those people?"

"Old surfers." Carmie pointed to Moondoggie and spotted her mom sitting on the blanket beside him. "Authentic."

Moondoggie was pulling off his wet suit vest. He shook his wet hair like a dog. "He was one of the biggest surf champions in the world," Carmie said. "He and my mom used to be boyfriend and girlfriend before my mom married my dad."

"Oh," Jenny said, stretching to get a good look.

"You know what that means?" Carmie asked.

"Your mom had a boyfriend." Jenny sounded disappointed.

"Exactly," Carmie said. "But not only that. My mom's old, really old boyfriend." She laughed. "Think about it. If my mom had married him, he could have been my real father."

"Whoa," Jenny said. Her voice got excited. "Your mom could have married a celebrity." Then she stopped, as if she was trying to seem bored again. "Is that the whole secret?"

"Not exactly," Carmie said as quickly as she could. "And Moondoggie just happens to be Coady's father. Get it?"

137

Jenny gave her a long look, like she was trying to figure the whole thing out. "Why is somebody's father called Moondoggie?"

Carmie's heart pounded. She had to think of something better for this secret quickly.

"Hey, little surf girl," Aloha Fats called. He held his baby high above his head. The baby's feet dangled in the air.

"Hey," Carmie called. She saw her mother hand a cell phone to Candy. Her mother stood up quickly from the blanket, where she had been sitting too close to Moondoggie. For a second Carmie felt proud. When her mom smiled, she looked like she did in the old pictures. Young and happy. Maybe *too* happy to be Carmie's mother.

"Hi, Elaine," Jenny called. "It's just us."

"Howzit?" Moondoggie smiled. "And who's-it?"

"I'm okay." Carmie laughed, walking Jenny closer. "This is my friend Jenny."

"Hello, Jenny." Moondoggie extended his hand to shake Jenny's.

"Hello." Jenny waved.

"Hi, sweetie," Elaine said, hugging Carmie. Her hug felt too strong, as if maybe it was fake. "I figured you'd know where to find me. Candy was nice enough to let me use her cell so I could call Aunt Raleigh."

"Oh." Carmie stopped.

"What happened to you?" Elaine laughed. "You're soaked again. You went in? Didn't I tell you? I hope you don't get sick! It's like ice out there."

"You should have seen her." Jenny seemed to be trying to

sound as if she felt comfortable being there. "I couldn't get out farther than my ankles."

"She can't help being that way," Moondoggie said, laughing. "It's in the blood. Like mother, like daughter."

"Yeah, I guess," Carmie said. She watched Jenny trying not to look at everyone.

"Is it time for me to go back now?" Jenny whispered. "It's okay, right? I'm definitely going to give Jon my aunt's number in Colorado and maybe I'll give him my e-mail address too."

Carmie thought as quickly as she could. Jenny could leave her there and go off and have a boyfriend. But without Jenny, Carmie would never be able to convince her mother to bring her back to the beach. Coady would not try to call her. For two weeks, Jenny would forget about Carmie. She'd be busy waiting for Jon to call her in Colorado if she hadn't already found a new boyfriend. Didn't Jenny even care that these were real celebrities she was looking at? "Just one last minute." Carmie pulled Jenny to the side.

"I haven't told you something that nobody else knows—"

"Hey!" Moondoggie called. "Where you girls going? Don't want to be seen with so many old people?" All the adults laughed.

"Wait up." Moondoggie ran to Carmie and Jenny. "This is Too Loose," he said, pointing to a man holding a guitar. "Duke of the Surf Guitar." Moondoggie laughed. "This bro is Chris 'the No Miss' Walker. You know Cotton Candy, Carmie. This is her old friend Little Lulu from Honolulu.

Lulu, this is Carmie and Jenny. You should have seen these ladies surf in their day, girls." Moondoggie smiled.

Little Lulu smiled at Jenny. Her skin was leathery tan all over. Her hair was even bushier than Carmie's, and she looked as if she was missing a front tooth.

"Hey, Romeo," Lulu said, laughing, "this is my day! Still breathing over here. Aren't I?"

"Nice to meet you," Jenny said, nudging Carmie to go. "Where do these guys live?" Jenny tried to whisper. "Are they homeless?"

"Homeless?" Moondoggie came closer. "Not me." He smiled at Jenny and patted Carmie on the head. "The ocean is my home. Has been all my life and always will be. But my house that I sleep in is about a quarter mile up from here." Moondoggie pointed toward the highway. "Right here in Malibu."

Jenny smiled. She looked at Elaine. Suddenly her face lit up. "Wow," she said to Moondoggie. "You have an actual house in Malibu?" She smiled at Carmie as if she was finally beginning to see what Carmie saw. "You must be rich. My mom and dad say they'd give anything if they could afford to buy a house in Malibu."

"Well." Moondoggie smiled.

"No, I mean it." Jenny talked loudly, as if she was relieved now that she knew she was safe. "My mom and dad sell houses. They always say this property is worth a fortune. You must be a millionaire."

Jenny watched Moondoggie and Elaine smile at each other as if they had a private secret. Then she pulled at Carmie's arm and ran with her, laughing, toward the shore.

"Do they like each other or something?" Jenny laughed. "Wait till I tell my parents I met somebody who has a house on Malibu Beach!"

"No, wait." Carmie stopped Jenny. "Shhh! You have to promise not to tell them."

"But why?" Jenny lowered her voice.

"Because." Carmie tried to look Jenny in the eye. Her brain was working so quickly she thought she might faint. "Here's the most important part of the secret. I haven't been able to tell you until now," she heard herself say. "It's not just that my mom and Moondoggie like each other. But I have some kind of bad news, too."

"What?" Jenny walked with Carmie. She pulled on Carmie's arm. "All right. What? I swear on my life I won't tell anybody."

"By the time you come back from vacation," Carmie said, voice trembling, "they will have made their decision."

"What decision?" Jenny sounded frightened.

"I didn't want to tell you," Carmie said. "Because I didn't want you to be worrying about me when you're in Colorado. But my mom says this could be her last chance. She and Moondoggie might decide to live together. My mom wants us to live out here with Moondoggie before they get married. I think I may be going to Malibu High."

Chapter 20

Carmie sighed and put down her movie notebook. For the first time since the famous movie scriptwriter had come to her school the year before and she had decided she wanted to be a screenwriter, she didn't know what to write. She looked at her clock. It was ten on a Saturday night, too late to call Jenny again. By the time Carmie woke up the next morning, Jenny would already be gone. Jon would call Jenny, but Coady would never call Carmie. Aunt Raleigh would be mad at her for not telling her mom that Aunt Raleigh had called, and Fluff Bucket would run outside and get hit by a truck. Carmie closed her eyes tightly to make the whole picture go away. She wished she could find a good movie to watch on TV.

*   *   *

The sun was almost down. Carmie looked at her clock. It was almost eight, the day after they had gone to Malibu for the last time. Carmie had spent most of the day either asleep or watching television. Jenny was in Colorado. In twelve more hours Carmie would be back in orchestra rehearsal and her mother would be getting sad again, typing up the doctor's tapes. It was as if Malibu had never existed.

Fluff Bucket followed Carmie into the kitchen. The hallway was quiet. Carmie knew her mother had been sleeping all day too. She opened a can of Chicken and Fish Buffet for Fluff Bucket, then took a cold piece of spelt bread from the fridge and smeared butter on it. She tossed some protein powder on top for nutrition. If only someone would save her.

Carmie looked at the answering machine on the counter. She saw that the light was blinking fast, which meant somebody had called. It seemed to be blinking superfast, as if to say, "Special call, Carmie. Special. Urgent. Just for you." Carmie pushed Play.

"Honey? Are you alive in there? Are you guys asleep or did you get swept up by a big wave? All that driving must have been a little too much for you, Elaine, don't you think? I got your message, which was probably from the beach, because I couldn't hear a thing you were saying. And I guess Carmie didn't give you my message, which isn't much like Carmie, since I told her it was really important. Hmmmm."

Carmie's heart sank.

"So listen. The other day when you were at the beach and I guess you didn't have your machine on, Sharon called me from your office because she didn't know how else to get in touch with you. She said to tell you that you don't have any work tomorrow, so don't bother driving to Dr. Tash's office. I guess he's not going to have anything this week and maybe not next week

either because of some big conference he has to go to. I'm assuming you're out some money. I don't want you to worry. You know if that's going to be really tight, you'd just better not be afraid to let me and Roy know. And let me know that you got this message, will you please? Hey! The good news is you can go with me now to the Tofu Expo at the convention center."

"Not if I get to her first," Carmie said to the machine, and erased the message. She swept Fluff Bucket off the counter, skipped down the hall and opened the door to her mother's room.

"Mommy?" Carmie said softly. "Are you asleep? Wake up! I have something important to tell you."

Chapter 21

BEACH LEGEND MOVIE SCRIPT
By Carmie "The Wave Curler" Hoffman

In her Beverly Hills mansion, CARMIE HOFFMAN, eighteen, is packing up her final surfboard in a special surfboard box. Almost everything else is out of the house. It just doesn't make sense to keep both the mansion there and the one in the Bu. JENNY and JON are there.

CARMIE

Yeah. I've just got to win the Pipeline Masters again this one last year. Then I can give the prize money to my mom. I promise you, though, that as soon as she gets married again, I can come back to visit here in B.H.

JENNY

You mean you're just going to forget about me?

JON

Don't just toss us away 'cause you win the Pipe!

CARMIE
(laughing casually, sexily)
Dudes. What are you talking about?

Carmie watched her mother's face as she backed the car out of the driveway. Somehow just her knowing she was driving back to the beach made her look better.

"Mommy, I love you," Carmie said. "I really want to learn how to be a really good surfer. Like you were. Like you still can be."

"I'm glad you enjoy the ocean, sweetie," Elaine said. "Just enjoy it. You won't learn how to be a really good surfer in one day. Don't put too much pressure on yourself. The beach will be there next summer too. But you can learn the easy way what really good surfers know: that the ocean can be dangerous, too. You can get hurt out there."

"Uh-huh." Carmie looked out the window. She was smiling, thinking of Coady. Everything was in place. Carmie had called Aunt Raleigh back and said her mom had gotten the message for sure. She had asked her mom straight out if they could go back to the beach one more day so Carmie could learn how to surf, and her mom had said yes. All Carmie had to do was go to orchestra practice first and hope that Aunt Raleigh wouldn't call and try to change her mom's mind. Carmie loved her aunt Raleigh dearly, but she was starting to be a problem.

"So the question is," Elaine said, looking at Carmie, "are you practicing your viola at all?"

"I practice," Carmie said.

"As much as you practice your movie writing?" Elaine asked.

"Yesterday I couldn't even write in my notebook," Carmie said. "I didn't know how to start."

"What's the matter with 'once upon a time'?" Elaine asked.

"No, Mommy." Carmie laughed. "I told you. Movies never start with 'once upon a time.' "

Elaine pulled up to the curb of the school.

"Well, once upon a time, there was a girl," she said. "And this girl had a lot of talent playing an instrument. And when she stopped playing her instrument and she got older and couldn't play anymore, she really regretted it."

"I know," Carmie said, getting out of the car. "You'll be here at noon, right?"

Elaine nodded and Carmie headed to the music room. She felt happy, waving back to her car. She thought of the story her mother had started. Why couldn't her mother just admit she was telling Carmie the story of her own life?

Chapter 22

"Thongs!" Elaine called as Carmie started down the beach. The sand was already scorching. The good news was that it was already almost one o'clock and the beach wasn't totally packed. Monday. It was just the locals again. Carmie smiled, dropping her flip-flops to the sand and sliding them onto her feet. She felt her jeans pocket for her cell phone and tied the bottom of her T-shirt like a halter top. She looked at all the beautiful Malibu girls stretched out sunbathing on their towels. The Malibu girls might not be looking at her, but they weren't looking at Jenny, either.

"That is a good-looking wave," Elaine said, smiling at the ocean. "If anyone had told me a month ago that I'd be back here again all these days in a row, I would have said they were crazy."

"Me too." Carmie pretended to laugh. A beautiful wave crashed. "This place almost feels like home."

"Mmm." Elaine smiled. Carmie checked to see if her mom had even heard her. Elaine was beginning to look almost pretty. Then Carmie's heart skipped. She could see the blanket of the legends, and Coady standing in his wet suit, looking out at the water. The rims of his glasses were glistening in the sun. Coady was the most beautiful boy Carmie had ever seen.

"Hey! Awesome!" Moondoggie called. "Look at these two beautiful ladies." His smile was enormous. "You can't stay away." He gently brushed Elaine's hand as he took her bag from her.

"I guess not!" Elaine said, then laughed for a long time. "My daughter wants to surf."

"Great!" Moondoggie said. "You going to go out with her?"

"Not today." Elaine laughed. "Not me."

"That's okay, Mom," Carmie said. "I know enough stuff. I can go out there myself." She didn't want Coady to think she had come back there depending on him to make her day. She tried hard not to look at him, but it had been two days since she had seen his face. The day she'd almost drowned, he hadn't seen her. Or had he?

"Coady!" Moondoggie called. "A couple of manners over here, dude."

"Hey!" Coady walked closer. "Hi, Elaine."

"Hello, honey," Elaine said.

Carmie liked the way her mother's voice sounded when she said "honey."

She called Jenny honey, and Aunt Raleigh, and other people, but not anybody she'd just met.

"How about taking Carmie out?" Moondoggie said. "It's pretty laid-back out there."

149

"Yeah, but it's cold," Coady said.

Carmie looked at the windy ocean. Coady was trying to get out of helping her.

"That's okay," Carmie said.

"Far out," Candy the Cotton Candy Rip Curler said. "You got your bathing suit on under those jeans today, don't you?"

"Uh-huh," Carmie said.

"Well then, hey!" Candy called out. "I got my old O'Neill here today. I'm not going to use it. You're not that much smaller than me, Carmie," she said, holding it up. "That's okay with you, isn't it, Elaine?"

"Is that what you want, sweetie?" Elaine asked.

"Of course it's what she wants," Moondoggie said. "The girl's got surf stoke. You remember what that's like, don't you?" He gave Elaine a long, slow smile.

"Just take it up to the bathroom and put it on there," Candy said. "You can put it right over your bathing suit. This is a really old one, so it doesn't have a zipper down the front. Just pull it down over your head like a tight sweater."

"Sweetie, do you want me to come with you?" Elaine asked.

"That's okay," Carmie said. "Just hold on to my cell." Carmie took her phone out of her pocket and tossed it high so everybody could see it.

"No worries," Carmie said, heading for the bathroom. "No worries."

* * *

150

Inside, the bathroom was empty and the floor was covered with dirty wet sand. The stall was small, and there wasn't anyplace for Carmie to hang her jeans or her top, so she let them drop to the floor. She held the wet suit out in front of herself. She was afraid to let it drop to the floor, because it was so heavy, like old jelly, and she was afraid she wouldn't be able to lift it up again. She stuck her ankles through the hole of the wet suit bottoms and then pulled them up over her butt with all her might. She jumped up and down. Every inch of her legs and stomach was sucked into the rubber. She was halfway there. She couldn't breathe straight, but it wasn't so bad. She lifted the top to put it over her head. The rubber wouldn't budge. She took a breath and tried again. She remembered Candy saying to pull it down over her head like a tight sweater.

Carmie held the neck. She tried to roll it. "Just pull it like you did the bottoms," she said out loud. She used both hands to yank the rubber over her head again. It got down to her eyebrows. She took another breath. She tugged the wet suit down over her nostrils. If it wasn't for her mouth, she wouldn't be able to breathe.

"Come on," Carmie muttered, pulling again. The wet suit came down, stopping on her nose and mouth. Carmie panicked. She could still breathe, but she needed to cry and there wasn't a place for tears to roll down. She tugged and the muscles of her arms trembled. Then the rubber slid and stopped over her mouth and below her chin. Carmie breathed. The rubber landed across her Adam's apple. She tried to scream, but no sound would come out. What difference did it make if she could? Nobody was there to hear her anyway. Carmie couldn't believe this was happening, but she knew what this was. This was her last moment on earth. Her last second of life.

Just then she heard the sound of flip-flops on the bathroom floor and then the hand dryer starting. She pictured a beautiful Malibu girl holding her perfect wet blond hair up to it. The girl was going out to surf. She had her whole life ahead of her. The dryer stopped. "Help me," Carmie gasped. "Oh God, please help me."

"Carmie?" a voice called from outside. "Sweetie, are you okay in here?"

"Mommy!" Carmie cried through her teeth. She turned around and threw her butt against the stall door. The door flew open and Carmie fell into her mother's arms.

"Get it off of me," Carmie struggled to say. "Mommy!"

"Oh, for goodness—" Elaine dropped her purse on the floor. "Just let me. Don't worry, sweetheart. I'm here." Elaine held on to both sides of the rubber and yanked quickly down over Carmie's neck.

"I almost had it," Carmie cried.

"Yeah, well, these old wet suits aren't so easy. I told you the ocean can be dangerous," Elaine said. She pulled the heavy rubber over Carmie's chest. "You need a wet suit with a zipper. There," she said. "Take a deep breath, sweetie. You're okay."

"How are you supposed to walk in this thing?" Carmie tried to laugh, but she still felt panicky. "It's so tight. Do I look completely fat?"

"No," Elaine said. "You look completely adorable."

"Can you do me a favor?" Carmie asked. "Don't tell Coady what happened. Okay?"

"All right," Elaine said. "It will be just between you and me." She smiled. She looked almost young again.

"Thank you, Mommy," Carmie said. "I'm going to go out first. Okay? Then you come."

Carmie headed out of the bathroom. The sun was shining and the ocean was straight ahead. She looked at her feet. They had the toes of a surfer girl in an old O'Neill. Carmie flattened her hair with her hand. She was alive.

"Go for it, Malibu Carmie!" She heard Moondoggie and Aloha Fats cheering her on from the blanket. She saw that Coady was waiting for her, and her heart started pounding.

Carmie looked at the ocean. The little waves were like glass, crashing ahead, and she was waddling like a stuffed baby seal.

It was too late to go back now. She had to do this so that her mother could get back together with Moondoggie. Someday her mother would realize that Carmie had saved her life.

Chapter 23

"I think I'm ready for the big stuff," Carmie said, following Coady.

Carmie watched Coady's smile, and his eyes focusing on the water. It was as if he knew every move of the ocean, every angle of the waves and every seagull that flew over them. He had lived all his life looking at the horizon. For Carmie, the horizon had always been the park pool and Fashion Square Mall. Until that summer.

Coady walked ahead. He steadied the board in the whitewater. He was just waiting for her. The water was like ice, and it made Carmie jump until it got up past her ankles. Then the thick rubber snake that had tried to strangle her before wouldn't let the cold come in.

"Hey, thanks, dude, for taking me out again," Carmie said. "I guess it's what our parents want. You're so lucky you have the dad you have."

"Hey! You want to see something?" Coady called, as if he hadn't heard a word Carmie had said. "Come here."

"Great!" Carmie tried to move more quickly. The wet suit made her bounce up and down in the water. Her feet could still touch the ocean floor. "Come on out farther," Coady called. "Don't be afraid. That's right. Just jump over those baby waves. Jump."

Carmie jumped closer.

"It's all about commitment," Coady called. "That's all it is."

Carmie smiled. Didn't she see this was it? Commitment was all it would take for her truly to be "Malibu Carmie." *Commitment* was also the word somebody said to a girl when he wanted her to be his girlfriend.

"You're doing great," Coady said when Carmie was close enough to see his face clearly. "A couple more feet." Carmie noticed something around Coady's neck. It looked like goggles.

"Have you ever looked under the water?" he asked.

"No," Carmie said. "I mean, only in the pool and maybe the bathtub. I'm better at writing screenplays than swimming. Did you ever see that movie *Blue Crush?*"

"Here," Coady said, laughing. "Goggles." He lifted the goggles carefully off his neck. "Want to?"

"What's under there?" Carmie asked. "Is it dangerous?" Coady gently put the goggles over Carmie's head and around her neck. Carmie could feel her heart beating in the wet suit.

"Now just drop into the water and open your eyes," Coady said.

"Just go under?" Carmie asked. She felt herself drop beneath the water. Below the surface there was nobody but her. Carmie and her heart beating.

"Open your eyes!" She could hear Coady's muffled voice. "Open your eyes."

Carmie's eyes opened and there was everything she had never been able to see before. A thousand fish and sponges in the most beautiful blue, all minding their own business, swimming under the spotlight of the perfect sun.

Carmie shot back up. "Oh my God! Do you know what's down there? I can't believe it!" She felt as if she might start to cry. "It's so cool. Don't you think?"

"Totally," Coady said. "Okay, quick!" He looked behind him. "Here comes a wave!" He held the board so Carmie could leap onto it.

"I did it better last time." Carmie tried to laugh and get her stomach on top of the board. "I think it's the wet suit."

"Okay now, remember to put your arms down to the sides. Like paddles. Good. You've got it."

Coady turned the board around. Carmie watched the beautiful muscles of his arms glisten outside his vest. She felt light all over. This was like a movie. Maybe even better than *Blue Crush*. Malibu Carmie was waiting for the exact right moment to leap onto the board. The wave curled over her and around her like a giant tunnel, and there she was standing on it, riding it, in the middle of it. Her hair soaked and totally straight. Commitment.

"Okay now, paddle," Coady said. "I'll push. You paddle. Paddle! Paddle!"

Chapter 24

"How long was I out there, Mommy?" Carmie asked as they turned left off the Pacific Coast Highway and back up the canyon.

"Oh, I don't know for sure," Elaine said. Her voice sounded strong. She checked her rearview mirror too many times. "Maybe thirty-five, forty minutes."

"Is that, like, a baby amount of time out there?" Carmie asked.

"Well, it's not so little," Elaine said, smiling. "We'll be lucky if we make it home in thirty-five or forty minutes. I would say you did very well considering you haven't gotten up on the board yet."

"The word is *yet*," Carmie said. "I bet I would be ready to try standing up on the board tomorrow."

"Tomorrow?" Elaine laughed. "Tomorrow is a good day to be ready to go to orchestra practice."

"But I don't have orchestra tomorrow," Carmie said. "Please, can we come back?"

"Well, Coady seems to be a very nice guy," Elaine said. "He seems to have taken a liking to you."

"It's all about commitment." Carmie tried not to blush. "That's what Coady said. Is that what Moondoggie says?"

"Oh, I don't know," Elaine said. "I suppose maybe he did once. I haven't seen these guys for a long, long time."

"Didn't you ever miss them?" Carmie asked. "They're fun. I miss Jenny."

"Well, this is a little bit different," Elaine said. "It gets different when you're older."

"Well, you don't have to worry," Carmie said. "Because your friends still like you. And besides, if it's still cold tomorrow, Candy said I can use her wet suit again. She is so totally cool."

"Right," Elaine said, watching Carmie. Then she turned on the radio. "Right."

FAMOUS MALIBU BEACH MOVIE SCRIPT
By Malibu Carmie Hoffman

Inside Carmie's mansion. CARMIE HOFFMAN is wearing a brand-new O'Neill full-body wet suit. It's all white with a racing stripe down the side of each leg that doesn't make her legs look fat.

MALIBU GIRL
You look so hot in that wet suit. I'm so jealous.
Where can I get one?

CARMIE
Don't worry. As soon as I get completely moved in, I'm opening my surf shop. I can special order yours. So you can bring everybody. Bring your credit cards.

Carmie heard something crash. She knew that her mother had been asleep for hours. Fluff Bucket jumped off the bed.

"Mommy?" Carmie called. "Mommy, is that you? Are you okay?"

"Sweetie?" Elaine called. "I'm just looking for something. I thought you were asleep. What are you doing up?"

Carmie's heart pounded. Her mother was in the hall closet. Her voice was still strong.

"I couldn't sleep," Carmie said. "What's in there?"

"Good question," Elaine said. "It looks like things have been sort of messed up."

"Oh," Carmie said. "What's supposed to be in there?"

"I didn't want to tell you," Elaine said. "I wanted it to be a surprise. If I even still have it."

"It's late, Mommy," Carmie said. "Aren't you tired? I don't want you to get sick. Well then, okay." She pretended to yawn. She started back to her room. She listened to the sounds of her mother in the hallway closet. She waited to hear her mother start back down the hallway to her own room before she got deep enough into the box to notice that the photos had been touched. Then Carmie heard her mother's footsteps come down the hall and stop in front of Carmie's door.

"Carm?" Elaine said softly. "I found it. I found my wet suit vest."

Chapter 25

"Listen to this!" Elaine said the next morning. She started the car. "I found this last night too. This used to be, like, the classic surf anthem." Elaine stuck a tape into the player.

Carmie laughed. "It must be classic. Those guys sound a thousand years old."

"Those are the Surfaris, my dear," Elaine said. "And I guarantee you they are only a hundred years old. You know. My age."

Carmie laughed hard. She couldn't remember the last time her mother had made her laugh like that. She looked at Elaine. Was this really her mother? Elaine's face looked bright and healthier. Her arms were a little tan and it made them look muscular.

"Good one, Mom," Carmie said. She was happy. If only this could stick.

"Can we stay all day?" Carmie asked when they turned onto the Pacific Coast Highway.

"Twenty-four hours?" Elaine asked. "You want to sleep out here too?"

"Could we? Well, it would save money on gasoline in case we decide to come back tomorrow, too. I think it would be so cool to sleep out on the sand."

"I think it would be so cool to sleep in a house." Elaine laughed.

"Cool." Carmie smiled. She hoped that day would be the day Moondoggie would invite them in.

∗   ∗   ∗

"Surf's up," Carmie called to her mother as they walked onto the sand. The waves were tiny. The air was warm and windy. Carmie straightened her hair with her hand. She was wearing her cleanest pair of blue jeans and her pretty pink top. After walking in that wet suit the day before, she almost felt like a real Malibu girl today when she walked. Three girls came toward her. One had red hair and two had perfect blond hair.

"We're just going straight to our spot, right, Elaine?" Carmie called loudly enough to her mother for the girls to hear. One of the girls nodded at Carmie. That was what being a local meant. Everybody had a secret code with everybody. But nobody was heading in the same direction as Carmie. Nobody was hanging out past the pier and on the beach blanket of the legends. And nobody was ever going to look like Coady. Nobody.

Carmie looked up and saw a pack of four surfer boys walking toward her. They were all wearing surf trunks and looking at a girl on a beach towel who had the straps of her bikini top untied as if all she wanted was to get a better tan. The boys all had surfboards. They all had blond hair. But only one of them had hair so blond it was white.

"Hey, Jon," the girl said, slowly. She looked as if she had to be a junior or a senior. "Where've you been hiding out?"

Carmie looked down. What if Jon remembered her mother? She needed to get her by him fast.

"Girls," she heard Jon say. "Hey. It's been kinda flat out there, so I haven't been around as much. But I do believe a set is coming in," he went on. "You want to come with? Sure is lonely without someone to watch me."

Carmie walked as quickly as she could. She felt sick. She could never tell Jenny. But Jenny's mother was right: when a guy really liked you, he wasn't afraid to say the word *commitment*.

*   *   *

"Hey," Moondoggie called. "Welcome home, girls. Surf's up!"

"Hey," Carmie called. She saw Coady sitting closer to the water. He was just sitting there looking at the ocean. That day there were more people on the legends' blanket, but none of them were as young as Carmie, except for Aloha Fats' baby.

"Say hi to baby Kuana." Aloha lifted the little boy above his shoulders. That day Aloha was there with his wife. Carmie had never seen Aloha with the baby's mother before. The mother was almost as tall as one of the long-boards standing up in the sand.

"You must be Mrs. Aloha," Elaine said, smiling and reaching for the woman's hand.

"Sorry," Aloha said. "Elaine, Carmie, this is Cheryl."

"Hey," Cheryl said. "Nice to meet you." She took the baby and rocked him in her arms. "But I'm not Mrs. Aloha." She laughed. "I'm just Aloha's chick."

"We don't go for the whole marriage thing," Aloha said.

"Oh," Elaine said. Carmie tried to imagine what it would be like to know that your mother and father had never even been married, much less divorced. That your mother was just a chick. Her mind went blank.

"Well, you have a beautiful little boy," Elaine said. She sounded embarrassed.

"And you have a beautiful daughter," Cheryl said, smiling at Carmie. "I hear you're a surfer."

"Well, not exactly, yet." Carmie tried to speak loudly enough for Coady to hear her.

"She's going to be as good as her old lady," Moondoggie said, reaching for Elaine's hand. Elaine reached back. Suddenly Carmie felt very alone.

"And what's this?" Moondoggie laughed. He reached into Elaine's beach bag and pulled out the old surf vest.

"Choice!" Cotton Candy called. "I remember that thing. You going back out?"

"This is for Carmie to wear if it's still cold," Elaine said.

"It's not bad today," Candy said. "You can get away with a vest or even nothing."

Carmie looked at Coady, thinking of what "nothing" was.

"I'm still cold from yesterday," Carmie said, as if she really meant it.

"Hey!" Coady called. He jumped up from the sand. "It's starting to pick up." He grabbed his board. He smiled at Carmie.

"Wax," he said, taking his surf wax out of his pocket. He waxed the board. "Necessary," he said. Then he started toward the water, holding his board on top of his head. His muscles looked smooth and shiny.

"You should have held on to one of your sticks, babe," Moondoggie said to Elaine. "You had a classic Jacobs board. Your sister had one too. Didn't Raleigh?"

"I guess," Elaine said with a laugh. "Frankly, I don't remember."

"Here," Aloha said. "Take mine. I'm not going out. It's plenty long. Takes the waves real mellow."

"Long enough for the both of us, sweetie," Elaine said to Carmie. "Come on. Let's go together. We won't go out too far."

"Okay." Carmie tried not to sound disappointed.

"You want my wet suit again, Carmie?" Candy asked.

"Yeah, that would be good. Thanks," Carmie said. "Are you wearing your vest, Mom?"

"Yeah, as long as I have it." Elaine laughed. "See if I can still fit into it!"

Carmie took Candy's wet suit.

"I'll meet you up there in just a couple of minutes," Elaine said to Carmie.

Maybe Carmie would be the only person in the ocean that day with a full-on wet suit. Maybe Coady wouldn't even notice. For sure Carmie would be the only one out there with her mother. How was any of this supposed to work out right?

"Hey, wait up!" a man called. Carmie looked behind her. Moondoggie was running over the sand. His legs looked strong and young for somebody's father.

"I'm going to the same place as you," Moondoggie said with a laugh. "Only I won't go into the girls' room."

"Great." Carmie tried to laugh.

"I'm totally stoked I'm going to see you and your mom on that gun," Moondoggie said.

"It should be interesting," Carmie said. She had never been this close to Moondoggie before. She was afraid he would say something about Coady.

"What's a gun?" Carmie asked quickly.

"You know," Moondoggie said. "It's another name you call a longboard, which is what it is."

"Now I get it." Carmie laughed. She started to walk into the women's room.

"I haven't seen your mom surf in a long, long time," Moondoggie said. "And there should be some action out there today. Coady's already got his space out there in our lineup," he said, as if he was proud.

"Uh-huh," Carmie said. She looked down.

"And I've got to get out there so he doesn't try cutting me off," Moondoggie said, laughing.

"You're going to go out too?" Carmie asked too quickly.

"Oh, sure, dude," Moondoggie said, as if it went without saying. "This is it, cutie. A little surf, Coady and an easy sight on the eyes with you and your mom right beside me.

165

How bad is that?" He looked Carmie right in the eye. His eyes were saying, "Your mom and I were meant to be together. I'm going to kiss her. Do you have a problem with that?"

"That's cool." Carmie smiled. "No, that's awesome."

Chapter 26

✳
     ✳   ✳
   ✳   ✳

"Cowabunga, man!" Moondoggie called out. He grabbed his board.

Moondoggie's friend Too Loose was sitting on the blanket, playing his guitar. "Give us a riff, bro." Moondoggie laughed. "We need some music to ride the wild surf."

"Dig it," Too Loose said. He plucked the strings faster than anyone Carmie had ever seen. "Remember this?" He laughed. "King of the Surf Guitar."

"Oh, wow." Elaine zippered her vest. "Dick Dale! Remember when we went to hear him, Sean?" she said to Moondoggie. She threw her head back as if she was about to laugh harder than she ever had since she saw the King.

"In Costa Mesa." Moondoggie pretended to chase Elaine. "Are you kidding? With you and your sister in my old VW van? You think I'd forget that?"

"Do you remember how to jump up over the waves in the shallow water?" Carmie chased after Elaine as quickly as she could in the wet suit.

"That's right," Elaine said to Carmie. "You know the right thing to do."

"And then you just dive under them when you get too far out and you won't get rag-dolled," Carmie said.

"Rag-dolled?" Elaine laughed.

"Yeah, you know," Moondoggie teased, "shredded, diced and sliced by the waves, man."

"What do you know, daddio?" Elaine laughed. "Come on, sweetie," she said, pulling Aloha's board out of the sand. "You take that end, I've got the other."

"It's too long," Carmie said. "This thing won't work. Coady's is better."

"No worries, dude," Elaine called out. "I am the cat to shoot this curl."

"Huh?" Carmie laughed. "Is that how they talked a hundred years ago?"

"No, I believe they used to say that when the dinosaurs roamed the earth," Elaine said, laughing. "Follow me, my little surfer girl."

Carmie and her mother ran to the shore. Carmie felt as if she was running through a dream. A dream in which this was really her mother. In the distance, Coady perched on his board like a beautiful hawk preying on the surf. Carmie understood now. He couldn't help it. He was just waiting for the perfect wave. The perfect wave and her.

The water was bright blue. The surface looked shiny, like glass. Moondoggie dropped his board into the water in front of him and paddled. His arms looked strong and nothing like Carmie remembered her father's arms looking when he took her to Santa Monica.

"This could be righteous," Moondoggie called over his shoulder. Carmie could feel her mother wanting to catch up with him.

"Well?" Elaine smiled at Carmie. "Want to hop on and paddle?"

"I think I can do it on my knees this time," Carmie said. "Just hold it." Elaine steadied the board. Carmie jumped onto it and then rolled off into the water. She tried again.

"Here, Carmie," Elaine said. "Get on your tummy first and then sit up on it with one leg on either side of the board. Like this." She showed her. She could do it almost perfectly. Then she rolled off the board and dunked under the water to warm up.

"This board doesn't work right," Carmie said. She watched Coady to see if he was looking at her. "I could do the knee thing on the other board."

Carmie looked at her mother's face. She had seen it in the pool before, but she had never seen it wet like this. Her mother's brown eyes were completely clear and alive. It was as if they were from another world—the one underneath the water that Coady had let Carmie see through his goggles.

"Are you happy, Mommy?" Carmie asked.

"Happy?" Elaine asked. She seemed embarrassed, as if nobody had ever asked her that question before. "How could I not be?" She smiled. "I'm with you. I'm stoked."

For a second Carmie felt so happy, she was afraid she would start to cry and make a fool of herself. Then Elaine turned and looked behind her. Waves were starting to roll in off the wave escalator at the end of the ocean.

"Elaine!" Moondoggie paddled ahead. He held on to the sides of his board, gliding up one tiny wave and then down to the other side. His board drifted farther and farther out. Coady was perched and ready, as if he was waiting for Moondoggie.

"We could catch up, Mommy," Carmie said. "Don't you want to keep going out?"

"This is far out enough for you and me," Elaine said, smiling. "I'm guessing that's not going to get too big but I still want to wait and see what the wave looks like. The waves are beautiful, but the ocean can be dangerous if you don't know what you're doing."

"But I know what I'm doing," Carmie said. "I don't just need the baby waves." She sat on the too-long board. "I don't need a baby's Boogie board." She noticed the flow of the ocean getting different. She felt nervous, held the sides of the board and slid onto it on her stomach.

She looked behind her. Moondoggie was standing up on his board. "He took off too early," Elaine said. "He's going to get pounded. Come on, quick!" Elaine turned Carmie around on the board, facing shore. "On your tummy. Paddle hard! Paddle! Paddle!"

"Yeeeow!" Carmie squealed. She couldn't tell if the wave or just her mother had pushed her, but she was riding. She was riding fast on this longboard, like an airplane cruising into the whitewater, until there was nowhere left to go. Carmie fell into the shallow water. The longboard rushed off ahead.

"Don't try to lift it," Elaine called to Carmie. "Wait. I'll help you. We'll turn this around together."

"No problem," Carmie called when she finally caught up with the longboard. She struggled to turn it around. The water felt so light, but the board didn't want to move back into the deep water. She looked at Coady to make sure he wasn't watching her. Then she saw something that almost took her breath away. Coady was standing on his surfboard. He looked like a god. The wave curled over him like a crystal tube and chased him.

"Come, let's push this dinosaur out there," Elaine said, putting her hand on the longboard. "You ready for another ride?"

Carmie kept her eye on Coady. She watched him glide up the side of a wave and disappear at the top. Then his board reappeared on the other side. He was going farther and farther out to catch the best wave. Carmie looked at her mother. Was it too late now for them ever to catch up? Could they ever be good enough?

Carmie watched Coady and Moondoggie cross each other on another beautiful wave. And then another. She watched her mother watching. "Elaine!" Moondoggie called. "Come on out here! Come on."

Carmie saw Coady fall into the water. Then he appeared again. He was coming toward them, and her heart started to pound.

"How long do you think we've been out here, Mom?" Carmie asked. "An hour? Do you think this is the longest I've ever been out here?"

"Hey," Coady called. He was getting closer. Carmie could see his eyes smiling behind his glasses. "Elaine, you want to use my board? Sean said he wants you to surf with him."

"He did?" Elaine looked toward Moondoggie. "I don't know." She looked at Carmie. "We've got the woodie here."

"I'll watch it," Coady said. "It's cool."

"You sure you don't mind?" Elaine asked. "What are you going to surf on?"

"It's okay," Coady said. "It's kind of small out there but the wave's got a nice little bite to it." He looked at Carmie. "I can show you how to paddle more on this thing if you want." He patted the longboard.

Elaine held Coady's board. It had a cord at the bottom of it. Elaine put the cord around her ankle. "It's like a leash," Elaine said to Carmie. "This is what you need when you get your board."

"Right," Carmie said, trying hard to sound as if getting a board was normal.

The sun was shining perfectly. It liked what it saw in the ocean. Moondoggie and Elaine could be husband and wife. This was one normal surf family.

"You were fantastic out there," Carmie said quickly.

"Oh, well, those waves aren't breaking very big." Coady laughed. "You know they break much better on the other side of the beach. But then there's a million guys down there and you're always getting snaked."

"I would hate to get snaked," Carmie said, as if she knew what *snaked* even meant. "I just want to stand up on this thing." She tapped on the longboard. Then she jumped on top of it and rolled off the other side.

"Nice," she said, coming out of the water. She pushed her hair away from her face. She tried not to look right into Coady's eyes.

"You're the most different girl I've ever seen," Coady said, laughing.

"Thank you," Carmie said. What did *different* mean, anyway?

"You're funny." Coady stopped talking. He reached up with his hand. He smoothed the hair off Carmie's face, separating the thick pieces. "You're the only surf chick I ever met who was so into it she would learn how to surf on a longboard," he said softly. Then he leaned in slowly and kissed her wet lips. A wave crashed. This was the best day of Carmie's entire life.

Chapter 27

FAMOUS MOVIE SCRIPT
MALIBU, THE B.H. AND BEYOND
By Cutie Carmie H.

In front of the mansion of CARMIE HOFFMAN in Beverly Hills. Special guest star Carmie is wearing a tight and perfect-looking cream-colored dress. By her side is COADY. He is wearing his contact lenses today. They get into Coady's brand-new silver Mustang convertible. KIYA ROSE, KATY LEE, DAN and DAVID from The B.H. are all there.

KIYA ROSE
It's so cool your mom and dad are getting married. I wish we could come.

CARMIE
I'd let you come but unfortunately only the best surfers in the world are being invited. I couldn't even invite Jenny, even if she was back from Colorado in time.

COADY
(opens the car door for Carmie)
We'd better go, darling.

The camera follows them to a beach even more beautiful than Malibu. It has cliffs. A wedding is about to take place. ELAINE is wearing a beautiful white gauze wedding dress. MOONDOGGIE is standing beside her in white pants and a Hawaiian shirt. There are lots of famous surfers and all the legends from the legends' blanket and other beautiful Malibu people.

MOONDOGGIE
(to Carmie)
You're going to be like my daughter. Can you believe it?

CARMIE
I'm stoked. I can still go see my first father when I have to. Right?

MOONDOGGIE
Sure. If you ever want to leave here again. Which I doubt.

Coady smiles at Carmie. They are all like family now and they know it. But there's more.

COADY
(to Carmie)
You are the most special girl I have ever met.

ELAINE
(hugs Carmie)
If it wasn't for you, none of this could have happened. Look at me now. I'm not sick anymore! Can you believe it?

175

THE SURF RABBI/MINISTER

Dudes and dudettes, we're here on this awesome day to marry up Elaine and Moondoggie. Maybe later we will even marry up Coady and Carmie, because I don't think that's against the law. So if anybody knows a reason why these two shouldn't get married today, speak now or forever hold your peas.

The phone rang.

"Hello?" Carmie answered.

"And a hello to you," Aunt Raleigh said, laughing. "I didn't wake you, did I, honey?"

"No," Carmie said.

"That's good," Aunt Raleigh said. "I didn't think so. Your mom just called me."

"Do you want me to get her again?"

"No," Aunt Raleigh said. "It's you I want to talk to. Your mom told me what you two have been up to every day. And I just have to say, I'm not so sure I'm much in favor of this."

"Oh," Carmie said. She'd never heard her aunt sound like this before. Why didn't she want Carmie's mother to have a good time? Did she know some horrible secret about Malibu?

"But, hey, if you really want this, you can have it. Who am I to stop you?"

"My aunt?" Carmie asked. Was Aunt Raleigh just jealous? Did she secretly have a crush on Moondoggie?

"Don't worry. Uncle Roy already knows," Aunt Raleigh went on. "He's out in the garage now."

"Why?" Carmie asked.

"He's looking for my old surfboard," Aunt Raleigh said. "What else? Didn't your mom tell you she's borrowing it? I forgot I even had it until she reminded me. I told your mom you can just pick it up on your way out to the beach. It will be standing there right by the washing machine."

"Whoa. Cool," Carmie said. "I didn't even know for sure we were going back tomorrow. You should have seen her, Aunt Raleigh. She was totally cool out there."

"Well, that's fine, honey, but your mom didn't ask for the board for herself. She wants it for you."

"She does?" Carmie asked.

"That's an original Jacobs surfboard, my little beach bunny. You have to take care of it. Not like you do your viola. Don't go into some wave that's going to break this thing in half. I just want you to be careful. Make sure you put on the ankle leash."

"I will," Carmie said. "I'm learning how to surf like you and Mom did."

"Far out," Aunt Raleigh said. "Just swear on a stack of violas you won't do the stupid things to get out to the beach that your mother and I used to do."

"I will." Carmie laughed. "I mean, I won't. I promise. And I'll guard your board with my life."

"Just guard *you* with your life," Aunt Raleigh said. Carmie wasn't exactly sure what Aunt Raleigh meant.

"Mom is healthy and happier now," Carmie said. "You should see! She hardly ever gets tired. I think these friends are a good influence."

"That's wonderful," Aunt Raleigh said. "But she's had

this chronic fatigue disease thing ever since the divorce, you know. That's three years already. The doctors say with chronic fatigue there's no promising it goes away forever. We all hope it will, of course. But I don't want you to get your hopes up and I don't want my little sister to get any sicker, either. You'll keep an eye on her, okay?"

"Okay," Carmie said. She was too excited about getting her own board to think about it. "Do you want to come with us?" she asked.

"To Malibu?" Aunt Raleigh laughed. "No, not me, doll-face. There are some real weirdos out there. I'm going back to the Tofu Expo."

$*$ $*$ $*$

Elaine pulled into the Malibu Beach parking lot. The tail end of Aunt Raleigh's board stuck out the back of the station wagon.

"I am so lucky I have you as my mother," Carmie said. "I'm totally stoked. You won't regret coming back here. You'll see." She opened the back of the wagon. The board slid out easily.

"Want me to help you carry that?" Elaine asked.

"That's okay." Carmie held the board with its insignia turned out in front of her. In a second the board got heavier than it looked.

Carmie saw herself running with Coady from the ocean straight up to his house. They were leaning against the wall in his kitchen. Her surfboard was standing right beside them. Coady leaned in and kissed her.

Carmie's arms hurt. Two surfer girls walked up the shore. They were different from the regular Malibu girls. They looked cool and strong and tan in their bikinis. They each carried a regular-looking board with swirling colors and racing stripes down the middle.

"Hey," the first girl said to Carmie. She looked at Carmie's board. Carmie smiled. "Hey."

"Howzit?" The second girl nodded. "Is that yours?" She looked at Carmie's board too.

"Mm-hmm," Carmie answered softly.

"Awesome." The girl tried to get a better look. "You ought to come down there and surf with us sometime. I'm Jill. This is Robin. See ya."

"Great," Carmie said. "I'm Carmie. Nice meeting you."

Then she couldn't stop smiling. That day she was different from any surfer girl Coady had ever seen, but she was one of them. Carmie looked at her mother. She had her hair pinned up, and a few strands of light brown swayed back and forth across her face. She looked young. Maybe even younger than when she was married to Carmie's father.

In the distance Carmie could already see the famous legends' blanket and then the old long boards sticking up in the sand. She could see Candy and Aloha and Too Loose and then Moondoggie. She saw her mother's face light up from the side.

"What took you so long?" Moondoggie ran to meet them. He kissed Elaine quickly on the lips as he had in the old picture. Then he kissed Carmie on the top of her head.

"Far out!" He looked at the board. "Is that what I think it—"

"It's a Jacobs original," Carmie said.

"I know," Moondoggie said. "That thing is totally cherry. It looks like it hasn't gotten a ding in years!"

"It hasn't," Elaine said. Moondoggie and Elaine smiled at each other as if they knew a secret language. A language they didn't want Carmie to know.

"Is Coady here?" Carmie tried to ask as if she was just curious.

"He's sitting down by the water," Moondoggie said, pointing. "Wait until he sees that board. He'll freak. Do me a favor and go show him. Okay?"

"No problem." Carmie smiled. "I'll be right back."

She started down to the shore. She felt her newly growing calf muscles pumping to get her through the hot sand. These were the legs that were turning into Malibu legs. This was the heart that beat faster as soon as it knew Coady was in sight. The sun danced over his sleek shoulders and the muscles of his perfect back. Another guy was sitting on the sand beside him, waiting for the surf. He had on a sun visor and was smaller than Coady. He would think it was totally cool that Coady knew somebody who had a Jacobs.

Carmie could hardly wait to drop the board into the water. She realized that if she could get her cover-up unzipped all the way, she could probably step out of it while she kept walking. Coady would know she was totally ready to go for it. Commitment. Carmie saw her big legs trying to hide under the flower on the pocket, but today they didn't look so bad. She slipped the cover-up off her shoulder and her left side. She felt the hot sun on her skin. Then she saw something funny on the back of the boy sitting next to Coady. It looked like a thin string. Carmie got closer. It was the string of a bikini top. His sun visor sat on top of a pile of blond hair. Carmie couldn't stop walking. It was as if she was in a dream in which the rest of her cover-up fell to the sand before she could stop it. All she could see was Coady's back, and pink and lime bikini bottoms.

Just then Barb turned around and looked at Carmie.

"Hey." Carmie tried to lift the cover-up off the sand. "Sorry, I didn't know you guys were talking. I just came down here because your dad asked me to—"

"You mean Sean?" Coady's voice sounded serious.

"Right," Carmie said. "Moondoggie. He wanted me to come down here and show you this."

Why was Coady being so serious? Couldn't he see she was already dying just standing there? Did he have to re- mind her that in Malibu people only called their parents by their first names? What did he expect from her in such a short time? What made him even deserve to see her board anyway?

"Sorry." Carmie started to head back.

"Where you going?" Coady looked Carmie in the eye. "We're just hanging. I'm just waiting for it not to be so flat."

"Are you going to come with me, Coady?" Barb asked. She stood as if she was posing.

Coady stood up and walked over to the surfboard.

"Is this yours?" he asked.

"Well, almost," Carmie said. "It was my aunt's. I think she's going to let me keep it."

"Smooth." Coady ran his fingers over the insignia. "Look at this thing, Barb."

"Everybody is surfing down on the other end," Barb said. "Don't you want to come with me?"

"Maybe I'll see you down there later if it picks up," Coady said shyly.

Carmie tried hard not to smile.

"Okay, see ya," Barb said, as if she didn't care. She looked Carmie up and down. "Or I'll see you tonight. Right?"

"Sure," Coady said. "I guess so."

Barb walked down the beach, swinging her hips. Coady watched her. Then he looked back at Carmie.

"What is this?" Coady asked.

"It's one of the original Jacobs boards." Carmie tried to sound as if she could concentrate, but her mind was racing. Were Coady and Barb boyfriend and girlfriend? If they were, why hadn't he gone with her? Were they going to a party that night? She was never going to go to any party. So what if Coady had kissed Carmie once? What if later he kissed Barb a thousand times? Carmie wished she could just crawl under a rock. Then at least Coady wouldn't keep looking at her in her bathing suit.

"Want to take this out?" Coady asked, smiling at Carmie. "It's going to need some wax first, though."

"I suppose," Carmie said. She reached for her cover-up. She could feel the cell phone in her pocket hit her thigh.

If only Jenny could call her just at that moment. That would be so perfect. She would tell Carmie exactly what to do. Jenny would have the right answer.

"Yo!" Moondoggie called, running up the beach with Elaine. They were holding hands. Carmie swallowed hard.

"Dude!" Moondoggie called to Coady. "You're never going to see one of those again. That thing's been in Carmie's family for ages. Let cutie get out and paddle a little on this baby."

"Cool." Coady looked at Carmie, and Carmie imagined that he was finally getting that she came from a long line of surfing legends. She wasn't just some girl afraid to get her pink and lime bikini wet.

"This thing is so awesome," Coady said. He laid the board on the sand and rubbed it with surf wax. "I'll show you how to stand today," he said to Carmie. "Okay?"

"Sure." Carmie smiled.

"Have a good time," Elaine and Moondoggie said at the same moment, like the Doublemint twins.

"I can carry it," Carmie said, taking the board from Coady. "It's not that heavy. Besides, I promised my aunt I'd guard this with my life."

"Great," Coady said. He tucked the board under Carmie's arm. She followed him into the water. It felt cold against her skin. Coady was up to his knees and then his thighs. It was as if the ocean loved him and made it easy for him. He belonged to the sea.

Carmie let the board fall on the water, then looked at it wet for the first time. Little waves were coming in.

"Should you hold this steady for a second so I can get on it?" Carmie called to Coady.

Coady stopped and turned around. "You can do it," he said, smiling. "You know how. Put your hands on the board first. Remember?"

Carmie didn't want to remember. Nothing looked the same on Aunt Raleigh's board. She put her hands on the sides of the board and leaped onto it on her stomach. The board toppled.

"Let's try that again!" she said, laughing. She held the sides of the board with her hands again and leaped onto it. Then she used all her strength to balance herself on the board.

"You got it," Coady said. "You're a little surfer girl. Now just breathe and paddle out to me. Just smooth and easy. Paddle to me. Paddle."

The water was flat. Carmie tried to imagine that her arms were long and beautiful oars paddling her into Coady's arms.

"Cool," Coady said when Carmie got near. "There's a couple of baby waves coming in. Perfect. Here, let me show you on your board." Coady got on her board right beside her.

"What you want to do is stay on your board like this until you can feel the wave coming behind you. It's building, building," Coady said, as if there really was a huge wave behind him. "You'll start to feel the beginning of the wave curling over you. That's when you paddle hard. Paddle. Paddle. Then, as soon as you feel that wave is moving you forward, that's when you stand up fast." He jumped off his stomach and onto his knees like a sexy frog. Then he stood up. "Put your hands up first and then lean forward, like this," he said, toppling into the water. He bobbed up. His glasses were still on their chain. He shook his head. He took off his glasses and laughed.

"There wasn't enough wave there to keep my balance," he said. He was a real person again. Carmie could feel her insides melting.

"Okay, now." He put on his glasses as if he had dried them off and they were perfectly clear. "Here comes a little wave. Ready to go for it?"

"Maybe," Carmie said. The wave didn't look so little to her. Why couldn't Coady come over and help her instead of just standing there looking at her?

"Okay, get on your board," Coady directed her. "Good. Good. Okay. Here comes the wave. Not yet. Not yet. Okay, can you feel it building?" Coady's voice got excited.

"I think so," Carmie said.

"All right." Coady kept looking behind her. "Okay, paddle. Paddle. Come on!"

Carmie tried to paddle hard.

"Now!" Coady called. "From your stomach to your knees and then stand." His voice sounded excited but patient. "Jump up now!"

Carmie held on to the sides of the board for dear life. The wave broke over her.

"I didn't get the 'now' part right," she said, drenched. She watched Aunt Raleigh's board run ahead through the whitewater.

"That's all right," Coady said, standing still.

"I'll get it!" Carmie called. Why didn't he go after the board this time?

"Doing great. Doing great. Paddle to me, paddle to me," Coady called. Carmie saw his eyes smiling at her. If she could just make it this time, he might kiss her on the lips.

"I think we'd better put your leash on you," Coady said.

"I guess," Carmie said. She could reach out now and almost touch him. She tried to stop breathing hard.

"Here," Coady said. "Jump off." He lifted the board high, straightening out the ankle leash on the end of it. "Put your leg up," he said.

"I can't get it that high." Carmie laughed.

"Then just keep it lifted," Coady said. He dived into the water. Carmie felt him grab her ankle. What did he see when he looked at her under the water? Her heart pounded.

"There." Coady bobbed back up. He smiled as if he had done this a hundred times. "Okay, now up on the board. Here it comes. Paddle. Paddle."

"Now?" Carmie cried out. "Now?"

"Yes, now!" Coady shouted. "Now, Carmie! Now!"

Carmie pushed herself up off the board with all her might. She felt as if she was in a movie in which she was fighting for her life and she was almost too tired to care if she won. Then she felt herself move. She felt herself rise. She heard the wave taking her over and then under the water, where there were only her and the sound of her heartbeat. And then a pound. A pound on her head that sounded like her head hitting rock. The leash tugged on her ankle. Then the board raced back. It hit her again on the head. Harder. Meaner. Aunt Raleigh's cool board had turned on her and was out to kill her. Now it wouldn't leave her side.

The water rushed over her until finally she could see sky. Her feet reached for the ocean floor and found it. She felt her head for gushing blood.

"That was better," Coady called. His voice was excited. "Here comes another one. Believe me. You'll get it. You'll get it."

"I got hurt," Carmie called, walking toward him. "I got hit with my own board. How lame is that?" She tried to laugh. She was too shocked to cry.

"You okay?" Coady asked. He looked at her head; then he touched the board. "These things can be brutal," he said. "Beginning surfers get hit a lot. But even the pros get hit sometimes."

"Oh," Carmie said. "This is really embarrassing, but I have to go to the bathroom."

"That's cool." Coady looked at her as if he just assumed she would pee in the ocean.

"I'll be right back," Carmie said. She turned the board around. She hated it now. It felt like a dead whale in the water.

"You sure you're okay?" Coady asked. "You want me to just park on that board here?"

Carmie thought of Aunt Raleigh. She would never have to know that Carmie had let Coady use her board. Plus, Coady would only like Carmie more for letting him use it.

187

"Okay." Carmie started for the shore. "Thanks."

"Hey!" Coady called. "I'll be waiting for you right here. I can't believe this board has just been sitting in your aunt's garage all this time. It so belongs out here. Like you."

"Yeah," Carmie said, smiling. "I guess you're right. You're just so lucky you're from here."

* * *

Carmie walked onto the beach. Her head felt light. She didn't know why she felt better just being away from Coady for a few minutes. But she did. She lifted her cover-up off the sand and put it on. Her cell phone rang.

"Hello?" Carmie asked softly.

"Well. Is the surf up?" a man asked.

"Daddy?" Carmie almost cried.

"How's my little surf bunny?" Her father laughed.

"I'm good," Carmie said.

"Wonderful," her father said. "Just as long as you don't become my little beach bum." He laughed. "Speak louder, honeybunch. I can hardly hear you. Where are you? You sound like you're in a tunnel."

"I'm practicing," Carmie said.

"Good. And I'm pretty sure I'm coming to the recital in a few weeks. My secretary is working on getting cheap tickets. Evelyn is going to come with me too. We're so proud. How's your mother?"

"She's doing really good," Carmie said.

"Oh, really?" Carmie's father asked, as if he couldn't believe the news.

"I'm watching out for her," Carmie said. "Like I promised. So you don't have to worry, Daddy. Daddy?"

The call was cut off. Carmie put the phone back in her pocket. She could feel her new calf muscles pumping as she walked in the hot sand. Her head was spinning. Coady was getting farther away. The blanket was getting nearer.

"Where's Coady?" Elaine asked. "Are you okay?"

"He's guarding the board," Carmie said. "I just have to go to the bathroom. So I thought I'd stop here first for a second."

"Righteous." Moondoggie gave her a big smile.

Carmie wondered where Jenny was in Colorado at that very moment. Was she thinking of her? Was she worrying about what it would be like if Carmie actually moved here? Carmie sat down on the blanket. She lay on her back and listened to the sounds of the pelicans cruising up and down the beach. She tried not to imagine Coady's eyes. Surfing was hard work.

Chapter 28

FAMOUS MOVIE SCRIPT
MALIBU CARMIE
By Carmie "The Curler" Hoffman

ANOTHER SCENE:
Outside at Malibu Beach. The big surf contest is about to begin.
Beautiful CARMIE HOFFMAN is carrying her Jacobs board down
to the water. She is wearing a perfect bikini with black and red
stripes. There are like a hundred girls competing.

GIRLS
(to Carmie)
Hey! Good luck out there, dude.

Carmie gives them each a high five. The waves are huge. About
fifteen feet tall. All the judges are sitting under umbrellas, and the
crowd is packed. Elaine and Moondoggie and Aloha and his
wife/girlfriend and Candy and Too Loose and Jon and even Barb
are there. COADY is sitting in the front. He gives Carmie a high

five. Carmie's heart melts, but she keeps her concentration. She paddles out. Farther. Farther.

COADY

Go for it, darling. You've got it! You've got it!

Carmie watches the water behind her. She paddles fast. Faster. She can tell that a lot of the girls are trying to catch the same ride. The time is right. Carmie stands up on the board. She puts her arm out. She steers the board to the right perfectly with her feet, racing ahead on the wave with gigantic power like you see in the movies. She's racing, racing.

"Are you ready to go?" Elaine called from the hallway. "If you really want to go to the beach again today, I want to see if we can't beat the traffic out there."

"Coming," Carmie called. She closed her notebook. She looked at her backside in the mirror. She deserved credit for going back and trying again at all, much less wearing her blue jean shorts and a blue top. Did she look too fat? If Jenny was there, she would tell her she didn't look too fat.

"Will you feed your sister?" Elaine called.

"Okay," Carmie called.

"And grab something to eat from the refrigerator for yourself. I went to the store."

Elaine's voice was happy and strong, like a sergeant's, and that made Carmie feel happy too as she smoothed her hair with her hand. Fluff Bucket followed Carmie to the kitchen. Carmie opened the refrigerator. She looked twice. Right beside the Chicken and Fish Buffet was a box of Extreme Power Treats like they had on the commercials. Carmie lifted a vanilla and strawberry power treat out of the box with one hand like in the commercials, in which the hungry person was always beautiful, active and on the go.

"Enjoy your final buffet in this place, Fluff Bucket," Carmie said, locking the door behind her. "I don't think this is our house anymore."

Elaine helped her slide Aunt Raleigh's surfboard into the back of the station wagon.

"Tasty!" Carmie waved the power treat.

"It's not as healthy as a hard-boiled egg and some wheat germ, but it still has plenty of vitamins and minerals," Elaine said.

Carmie looked at her mother. She had pink lipstick on and her bathing suit top was peeking out her shirt. Carmie had never seen her mother's bathing suit peek out of any shirt before. Her mother's skin had turned a soft tan. She looked almost like a surfer girl.

"Did Dad tell you he's trying to fly in for your recital? I got an e-mail from him this morning. He and Evelyn might both be coming."

"That's what he said," Carmie said, watching her mother drive. Her smile looked as if it was coming down.

"Maybe Moondoggie will invite us to come up to his house today," Carmie said enthusiastically.

"Well, maybe," Elaine said.

"You like Moondoggie. Right?" Carmie asked quickly. She looked at her mother again to see if she was smiling.

"It all depends on how you're defining *like*," she said, as if she was repeating something serious from one of the medical tapes.

"You know, Mom," Carmie said. "When two people like each other, they like to do things together and go out on dates."

"Well, Moondoggie and I like each other." Elaine smiled. "We are old, old friends. And we like to hang out at the beach together. But we're not exactly dating," she said, with the corners of her mouth turning slightly up.

"So then don't you want to go see his Malibu house?"

"I hadn't given it much thought," Elaine said, reaching over to tickle Carmie's stomach.

Carmie watched her mother drive up the canyon. She did not brake every other second on the curvy parts. Carmie had come too far to ever go back now. She had to do something fast.

Her cell rang.

"Surf's up, dudette," Carmie answered.

"You can say that again, dood-dah," Aunt Raleigh said, laughing. "Where are you?"

"Almost at Malibu." Carmie laughed.

"Well, I'm about to turn into the convention center. The tofu taffy tasting is just about to start. And they've got so many vegetarian guest speakers today. Are you listening to the radio? Tell Mom there's a south swell."

"What does that mean?" Carmie asked.

"It means be careful at Malibu. Surf is definitely up."

Elaine turned right onto the Pacific Coast Highway. The waves were crashing down as if they were in a big storm, even though the sun was shining.

"Wait until we get closer to the beach." Elaine's voice sounded excited. "Today we'll see Malibu in all its glory."

193

Carmie watched the waves climb higher and higher along the coast and crash back down again like angry roller coaster cars.

"Those are probably close to five feet," Elaine said. "Almost as tall as you!"

Carmie looked out the window. How was she ever supposed to stand up on one of these?

Elaine got the only parking spot in sight.

"The surf gods know we belong here." Carmie laughed, sliding Aunt Raleigh's board out the back of the station wagon. The ocean looked almost full of surfboards. It was like a circus of clowns in wet suits and shorts. A couple of guys in short royal blue wet suits led the way down the front of a wave. They looked like pros.

"See that guy there with the red trunks trying on the right?" Elaine pointed. "He's not ready for waves this big," she said, as if she was talking right to him. "He's taking off way too late. Prepare for a wipeout."

Carmie watched the guy fly facedown into the crashing whitewater.

"We should just go down to where Moondoggie is, Mommy. It's too crowded here. The waves will be better where we always are." Carmie lifted her board out of the sand. She hoped her mother would believe her.

"Well, I don't think so." Elaine followed. "Look, sweetie. Recognize these hotshots?"

Carmie saw two guys running up the beach, carrying a boat. As the boat got closer, Carmie saw it was really a gigantic board. Moondoggie was in the front. Aloha was carrying the back end. It was the longest board on the beach. Carmie felt embarrassed. People were staring and pointing.

"Hey, M.D.!" Elaine called more loudly than Carmie had ever heard her mother speak in her life.

"Hey, you beauties!" Moondoggie ran toward them.

"Ladies," Aloha called. "It's like the Pipeline out there today. We brought the gun."

"Come on, Elaine!" Moondoggie said. "Candy's out there. So are Too Loose and Chris and Honolulu Lulu. We've been out already for two hours with the groms. I've been waiting for you to show them how it's done." He laughed. That day Moondoggie looked different than he did on the legends' blanket. Older.

"Isn't anybody back at our blanket?" Carmie tried not to be obvious about looking at the water for Coady.

"Oh no. This is where it's happenin' today," Moondoggie said, reaching for Elaine's hand. "If you can fight your way onto a ride, the surf's worth it."

"We're the watchers," Elaine said. "And there's plenty of entertainment to watch. Besides, I don't have a board."

"Are you kidding?" Moondoggie looked at the Jacobs. "You'd let your mom borrow your ride, wouldn't you?"

"That's okay." Elaine put her arm around Carmie as if they were best girlfriends. "That board is Carmie's. And it's a little too gnarly for us beginners. Go on, go for it. Scat!" She laughed.

"All right." Moondoggie shook his head at Carmie as if he couldn't believe her mom was giving up a good time for her. "Well then, your job is to watch us and keep an eye on her for me. Don't let her run away. Don't let anything happen to your mom. Okay?"

"You can count on me." Carmie tried to sound helpful. Didn't Moondoggie know she'd already had to make that promise to her father?

Carmie watched her mother watching the ocean. "Are you sure you don't want to go out there, with Moondoggie? It's not like this isn't the coolest thing that's ever happened in our whole lives," Carmie said.

"You're the coolest thing that ever happened," Elaine said over the crashing surf, as if she had never said anything truer in her life.

"So are you," Carmie said, afraid she was lying and would start to cry if she didn't look away. She watched for Coady. If only she could spot his glasses and just see his eyes. How hard it must be for him to be out there with so many people who weren't real surfers.

"Hey, dudes! You're home!" Candy called, running out of the ocean with her board. She gave Carmie a wet high five.

"How is it?" Elaine asked.

"Insanity. But righteous." She looked at Carmie. "I'm done out there, cutie. You want my wet suit again?"

"That isn't any beginners' break," Elaine said.

"Well, your mom is right," Candy said. "It takes experience just to know how to deal with all those little hodads. Some kid went aggro on me because I wouldn't let him cut me off. It's a different world out there, Elaine." She smiled. "Who would have ever thought when we ruled that surfing would come to this?"

"Not me," Elaine said. "But it's still the same ocean."

"Well then, come on, girl," Candy said. "Take my board before the wave set."

"Well . . ." Elaine looked at Carmie. "You sure you're okay here, sweetie?"

"You can come back down with me to our spot," Candy said. "Bring your board. All I'm going to be doing is sleeping."

"That's okay," Carmie said. "Thanks."

Elaine took off her shorts and top, and Candy handed her the board. They looked at each other as if they knew a secret language. Then Elaine started for the shore. Carmie stood and watched her run into the shallow water until she didn't look like Carmie's mother anymore.

"Go for it, Mom," Carmie said softly. She took a deep breath. She had to make this happen.

"You still waiting for Coady?" a voice called. Carmie turned to see Barb walking toward her in her pink and lime bikini.

"Hi, Barb! I think he's out there," Carmie said, trying to sound helpful.

"Of course he's out there," Barb said, snickering. She fiddled with the edge of her bikini bottom as if she didn't know it wasn't covering her whole butt. "Where else do you think he'd be?"

"Good point," Carmie said, and laughed. A chill ran through her body. She tilted her surfboard slightly toward Barb so that Barb could see the insignia.

"You're a Val," Barb said. Her mouth crunched up like a crab's. "Coady's a beach boy. Why are you bothering him, coming to the Bu every day?" Then she turned and walked away before Carmie had a chance to answer.

Carmie stood there, her arms trembling. What would she have answered, anyway?

"Yeeeehiiii," a bunch of guys called from the ocean.

"Hey." A girl's voice came from behind Carmie. "That's that awesome board. Carmie, right?"

Carmie turned to see Jill and Robin, the surfer girls from the day before.

"Hey!" Carmie said. "Howzit?"

"Oh, man!" Robin laughed. "Come on out with us." She reached to give Carmie a high five. "You're not going to miss this with that ride. Are you?"

"I guess not." Carmie took off her shorts and top. She stacked them on her mother's. Then she pulled her board out of the sand. She knew it was dangerous, but she thought somehow she would be protected. She knew she would die for sure if she had to tell Jill and Robin the truth. Carmie looked down at the ankle leash on her board. Then she ran.

"My mom's out there surfing already," Carmie called, behind Jill and Robin. "She used to be, like, a legend."

Her feet hit the ocean. Some kids trying to wade in the shallowest parts laughed and squealed.

"This is a surfing beach." A lifeguard's voice came over a megaphone. "If you're not out there on a board, you don't belong out there in that water. Get out of the water now."

Carmie held on tightly to the Jacobs. Even the shallow water was trying to knock her over. She watched Jill and

Robin jump over the little waves. Then they were already too far out.

Carmie let the board drop in the water and fell on top of it as quickly as she could. A little wave knocked her over. She held her breath and grasped the sides of the board tightly. She knew if she let go of the board, she might never find it again. Under the water it was quieter and completely lonely. The wave turned her upside down and then up again on her stomach. She looked up. The fin of a board was headed right toward her face.

"Hey! Move out of the way!" a guy called.

Another board came fast toward her. It flew out from under the surfer boy and spun in the air before it hit the water farther away from Carmie.

The next second the lip of a baby wave approached. She could hear Coady saying, "Just hold the sides. Hold the sides and glide right over the top. Hold on tight. The ocean will take care of you. Don't be afraid."

"I'm coming," Carmie said. She gripped the board and tried to look up. The wave lifted her high to the sky and gently set her back down. All she could see in front of her now was an escalator of waves that stretched into forever. She paddled gently and held on to the sides of the board. She knew she was going too far out, but she didn't know how to turn the board around. She could see people taking off on the waves in the distance. One of them had to be her mother. If Carmie could just get to her, everything would be all right.

"Yeeehiiiiiii . . ."

"Hey, bro," a guy called. "You girls over there are going to get hurt out here. Don't you get it?"

"Get a life!" A girl flew into the water. "And while you're at it, get a different beach!"

A board raced toward Carmie's head, then veered to the left, as if it was slicing the water in half.

"All right!" A guy on a bright yellow board hooted. "All right! Thank you, ocean!"

Carmie tried to look up enough to see the surfer's face. His legs were sculpted and beautiful like Coady's. His voice was gentle and kind like Coady's. He looked like an angel sailing across the top of the water.

"Hey, a-hole," a guy screamed. All Carmie could see coming toward her was white-blond hair. Another guy came in off the left. He waved his arm as if he was ready to slug with it.

"You burnout! Consider yourself warned."

"You threatening me, dude? What are you, blind? Didn't you see me?"

"Yeah, I saw you," the first guy said. "Don't ever drop down on me again. You hear me? Just be glad my board didn't bust in half. You've got a bad attitude, man. Why don't you take it out of the water?"

"Oh yeah?" the second guy said. "Come on, man. You want to talk bad attitude to my face?"

For a second the water seemed still. Carmie paddled hard, keeping one hand in the water so the board might turn toward the shore. Then she stopped. She looked into the face of the guy with the white, white hair. It was Jon. She held on to the board and let the water turn her over.

Did he see her? He would look at her in her bathing suit and think she wasn't Jenny and didn't have a body hot enough to save. Carmie held her breath under the water for as long as she could. She was hating herself and trying to cheer herself on at the same time.

When the wave rolled her back up, Jon was paddling out toward the lineup. Then she saw the other surfer paddling out after him. Carmie froze. It was Coady. That day he wasn't wearing his glasses.

"Coady!" Carmie yelled.

Coady leaped onto his board. Carmie swallowed hard. What was she doing coming back to Malibu, anyway? What if Barb was right?

"Coady!" she yelled more loudly. For a second Coady glanced back, as if he hoped he heard Carmie. Then he put all his concentration into paddling.

"Hey, move out of the way, you geek!" a guy called.

"Thanks for snaking me, bro," another guy called sarcastically.

"All right!" A girl cheered from her board, finishing out her ride.

"Hey, girl with the black striped bathing suit," a guy called. "What are you doing? Trying to get killed? Get out of the way, you fool!"

"Sorry!" Carmie said, knowing no one would hear her. If only she could have called back, "What kind of an idiot are you if you don't know the difference between a Boogie board and a classic Jacobs?" If only she could see her mother. Even the seagulls were trying to fly away.

Carmie felt a baby wave coming behind her. She paddled.

She was too tired to paddle hard. But she had to get closer to shore. Any little distance the wave could move her would be better than nothing.

"Going my way?" a man called. Carmie tried to paddle out of the way.

"Hey!" the man said. "You're not going my way? Cutie! Wait up!"

Carmie looked behind her. Moondoggie was swimming. He didn't have a board. She hardly recognized him with his hair wet and flat against his head. Carmie felt nervous being so close to him. Was he thinking, "How did Elaine ever get a lame daughter like this? Why would my son ever like someone with a big red and black striped butt?"? Moondoggie reached out and touched the tail of the Jacobs.

Carmie was afraid to stop holding on to the board.

"Hey!" she said in her most laid-back tone of voice. "Have you seen my mom out here? These waves are a little intense for me."

"Me too," Moondoggie said, and laughed. "Aloha's six months younger than me. He can stay out there all he wants. I need some sustenance. Here." He held on to the tail. "You just relax." Moondoggie looked behind him. "I'll push us into the wave," he said. "Get ready. Feel it? It's coming. Now! Now! Now!"

"All right! All right!" Carmie hooted.

"Stoke me," Moondoggie called, hitching a ride on the back as if he was a tugboat.

"Thanks!" Carmie laughed. "You didn't see my mom out there, did you?"

"Don't worry about her. She's way out on the outside,

trying to catch a ride with Coady. We're just like one big happy family out here."

"Great," Carmie said. The sun was smiling on her. It was saying, "Chill. All your plans are going to work out fine."

"I'm starving out here," Moondoggie said. "Aren't you?"

"I guess." Carmie lifted her board from the water.

"I'm going up to the house and making us all sandwiches," Moondoggie said. "Help me?"

"Righteous." Carmie smiled.

She followed Moondoggie over the sand.

"Here." Moondoggie took the board from her. "Let me help you. I don't want you telling your mother I'm not a gentleman."

"Okay," Carmie said with a laugh.

"I'll tell everybody who even looks at this board that it's yours," Moondoggie promised, sliding the Jacobs under his arm. Then he put his other arm around Carmie. She smiled, thinking how lucky Coady was. Moondoggie must be such a cool father.

＊　＊　＊

"How you doing, Carmie?" Moondoggie asked.

"Great," Carmie said, following him as they passed the pier and then their blanket. Candy was on the blanket, fast asleep.

"Well, she'll be useless to guard your ride," Moondoggie said, laughing. "Come on, we'll take it up to the house."

"Cool," Carmie said.

Moondoggie pointed to the hillside cliff that led up to the highway. "It looks steeper than it is. Here, you go first."

Carmie had never been much of a climber. The hill looked too steep. She could hear the waves crashing behind her. They sounded beautiful.

"You're so lucky to live up here," Carmie said, struggling to catch her breath.

"Yeah, it's nice," Moondoggie said.

"My friend Jenny's parents work in real estate and they said the best houses are out here."

"Well, there's a lot of rich houses up here, that's for sure," Moondoggie said. "A lot of movie stars come here. I've been in the Bu most of my life, and in this pad a lot longer than most of them have been here. Since before you were even born."

"Was Coady born yet?" Carmie asked shyly.

"No," Moondoggie said. "Well, let's see, how old is he? I think he's sixteen. Or maybe he's still fifteen."

Carmie laughed at Moondoggie's joke. "Did you ever know my father in the olden days?" The words came out her mouth too quickly.

"Your father?" Moondoggie chuckled. "No, I didn't get to meet your dad. Or your aunt Raleigh's old man either. They all came after me. I was probably with, let's see, Rachel by then."

Carmie laughed. She wondered if Rachel was Coady's mom. Would Moondoggie really have to stop to remember her name?

"But I'm sure glad you and your mom are back now," Moondoggie said, helping Carmie up the final step. "She used to be quite the surfer, I'm sure you know. She was a lot better surfer than her sister, but don't tell her I said so. Anyway, she was away way too long."

"Tell me about it." Carmie caught her breath. She was happy to be on the top. The highway was lined with houses that faced the water. There were fancier cars than any of the Mustangs in the beach parking lot. There were no old stores you had to pass along the way like Silvia and Laticia's Leche, Carne y Dulces market in Van Nuys. There was not really much of a sidewalk. Carmie saw herself always running down the beach to get somewhere when they moved in.

"Only two more down, cutie," Moondoggie said. Carmie looked at the second house and her heart started to pound. It looked rich like all the other ones. A fancy red sports car was in the driveway.

"Whoa," Carmie said softly. "What is that? A Mercedes SL?"

"That's it." Moondoggie led the way down a path along the side of the house. There were pretty cobblestones with big flowerpots on the side. Carmie saw a dirty old blue Volvo with a bumper sticker on it that said "The Endless Summer." Carmie smiled. Someday soon she would ride with Coady in his car. This was the summer that could never end.

At the end of the path Carmie saw a little house, apart from the big house. She thought the little house must be where everybody went when they had just come off the beach.

"If I knew I was having company, I would have cleaned

up more," Moondoggie said, laughing. "By the time you and your mom come over for one of my famous abalone dinners, the maid will have been here."

Carmie stepped inside. She was in the kitchen. It was long and narrow with no real wall to lean her surfboard against. Milk, an egg carton with runny yolks still in the broken shells and a can of SPAM were on the counter. The sink was stacked with dishes. A half-full can of Chicken and Fish Buffet cat food was floating on top of the pile. Past the kitchen was one large room with rustic-looking wooden paneling and a fireplace. There were a table and chairs and one big round window, shaped like a porthole on a ship, that faced the ocean. Up high was a loft with a mattress on the floor and T-shirts and magazines hanging off the side.

"That's your friend Coady's personal pigsty." Moondoggie shook his head. "I'm going to put your board right here," he said, and took the board outside.

Carmie looked around. A bedroom door was half open, and she could see that the bed sat close to the floor. It was half made, with a lot of clothes on top of it. On the wall was a big framed picture of a short, wavy-haired blond cartoon character carrying a surfboard. The poster said "Cowabunga." A small desk with a computer on it sat in the corner. Carmie thought that was where her mother could do her medical typing.

"I like your house," Carmie said quickly.

"You can't beat the location." Moondoggie smiled. "It's pretty cool for a guesthouse. There's enough space for me. The people who live in the big house have got the huge digs and the boss car. They're Beverly Hills transplants."

"Oh," Carmie said, trying not to look as if she was completely disappointed that this was all there was. "Do you have a cat?" she heard herself ask. "We have one too. Fluff Bucket."

"Oh yes," Moondoggie said. "Princess Blue. She's around here someplace. She's Blue in the Bu. She likes to check the surf." He took peanut butter out of the refrigerator. "We always know exactly where she is when she meets up with the cat next door. Sheba doesn't play well with others."

* * *

From the top of the cliff, the climb down looked easier. It felt good to be back outside in the clean ocean air. Moondoggie carried the Jacobs high over his head. Carmie held on tightly to the bag filled with sandwiches.

"Look," Moondoggie said, pointing. "Here come your mom and Coady."

Carmie's heart fluttered. She saw Coady and her mom carrying their boards.

"Hi, sweetie!" Elaine called. She sounded proud and happy.

"Hey!" Coady called, looking right into Carmie's eyes. It was like a movie.

"How was it, Elaine?" Carmie asked.

"I'm stoked." Elaine waved.

"It's so good out there. A little radical, but she didn't bail," Coady said, chuckling.

"Of course she didn't," Moondoggie said. "Nobody bails

here. Carmie and me were just up at the pad making sandwiches."

"Hey," Carmie said to Coady. "I watched you out there before. I was trying to learn something." She went on. "You were awesome."

"All right," Coady said, smiling. He reached for the bag of sandwiches.

"Hey," Moondoggie said, grabbing the bag away from him. "Who raised you, brah? Where's your manners?"

"Sorry." Coady handed the bag to Elaine.

"Thanks, sweetie." Elaine handed the bag to Carmie. "Chefs first. How was it up there in the kitchen, Carmie?"

"Great," Carmie said. "It's totally great."

"I knew it." Elaine grabbed a sandwich and took a bite. Carmie had never seen her mother eat so fast before. She gave Moondoggie a big smile, and Carmie thought she looked pretty. Then she handed the bag back to Coady.

Coady pulled out a sandwich and sat down beside Carmie on the blanket.

"Hey, dude," Coady said to Moondoggie. "You ready?"

"You're going back out already, brah?" Aloha asked.

"Pretty much." Coady swallowed the last piece of his sandwich.

"You?" Moondoggie asked Elaine. "You want to hit it again?"

"I think I need to hit the road," Elaine said, smiling. "Frankly, I think I'm a little older than when I last surfed." Her voice sounded tired. "I'm a little sun knocked out here and we've got a drive back."

Carmie looked at her mother and her heart pounded.

"Are you okay, Mommy?" she asked, trying not to sound afraid.

"Snooze out for a bit," Moondoggie suggested. "You'll wake up refreshed and ready to roll."

"I don't think so." Elaine laughed. "Thanks so much for the sandwich."

Coady stood up and lifted his board from the sand.

"But, Mom," Carmie said. "This is like the best surf of the summer."

"It would be a hell of a lot easier if you just lived here," Moondoggie said, smiling at Elaine. "Huh?"

"Shorter drive for sure." Elaine tried not to smile back at him.

"But, Mom . . ." Carmie tried to argue without whining. "It would be better if you take a nap for a while before we go. Or I can go get you a Diet Coke. Remember the time you drank one of those things? It woke you right up!"

"Hey," Coady said, taking Carmie's arm. "Come back tomorrow, okay? The surf's still going to be really good. And if you can, tomorrow night there's going to be another party out here at some guy's house."

"Oh," Carmie said softly, completely surprised. Would Elaine ever bring her back if she knew Carmie just wanted to go to a party? How would Carmie ever get her mom to stay at the beach all day if she even got her to come back in the first place?

Carmie watched her mother talk to Moondoggie and Candy. Coady looked at Carmie again and smiled. Carmie's heart melted. "Cool," she said, trying not to blush. "All right. Tomorrow's great."

Chapter 29

"Are you okay, Mommy?" Carmie asked as they turned off the Pacific Coast Highway. She watched her mother's eyes from the side to make sure they weren't closing.

"I'm fine." Elaine checked the rearview mirror again. "I don't know what came over me. I just suddenly got so sleepy. Well, I guess I do know what came over me," she said, correcting herself, and smiled. "I'm not in shape for that kind of surf. I don't belong out there."

"Of course you do," Carmie said, trying to sound like a cheerleader. "That's why we just have to keep coming back. Tomorrow will be better. Practice makes perfect. Right? You'll see." Then she looked at her mother and stopped. Her mother wasn't responding.

"You're okay to drive. Right, Mommy?"

"Turn on the radio, sweetie," Elaine said. "Something lively."

Carmie's cell rang.

"Surf's up," Carmie answered.

"Are you alive out there?" Aunt Raleigh asked.

"Let me check," Carmie said, and tried to laugh. She looked at her mother. For the first time in a while, she looked tired around the edges of her mouth. "We're good," Carmie said. "And so is your Jacobs. Mom surfed today. The south swell is still supposed to be ripping tomorrow."

"Cool," Aunt Raleigh said. "Ripping, eh?"

"Does she want to talk to me?" Elaine asked. "Tell her I'll call her back as soon as I get home."

"Did you hear that?" Carmie asked. "I'm not forgetting to pass on this message. Right?"

"Righto, daddio," Aunt Raleigh said. "Tell her to call me as soon as she gets in the house, honey. Thanks."

FAMOUS MALIBU MOVIE SCRIPT
By Carmie "The Malibu Carmie, Rip Curler Cutie" Hoffman
DEDICATED TO F.B. (Fluff Bucket)

Night. Outside the entrance to Malibu Beach. The big party is about to begin. Beautiful CARMIE HOFFMAN gets out of COADY's newly cleaned and painted Volvo. It is such a cool car, because it's a classic, like the Jacobs board that is attached to the top of it. Carmie is wearing a sexy white short top and perfect matching pants. Her tan is smooth and almost perfect. Coady gets out of the car. He puts his arm around Carmie. Everybody is there, including Barb. She is by herself. She is wearing a pink and lime sundress that matches her bikini, because she doesn't have an original idea when it comes to dressing well. People are dancing on the sand and just hanging around.

211

COADY

Hey, everybody. Gather around. This is my girlfriend, Carmie. She's officially moving to the Bu tomorrow.

EVERYBODY

Hey! Hey, you two! This sounds serious!

Carmie looked at the word *serious*. Suddenly it hit her all over her body. This *was* serious. She was in the middle of a bunch of lies and she had to think fast to make sure she didn't get caught in any of them. Jenny would be home soon enough. What was Carmie going to tell her was the reason her mom and Moondoggie had decided it was better that they not move to Malibu? Carmie tried to come up with an excuse that sounded right. Jenny wouldn't believe any of them. Then Carmie brightened as she realized something. Jenny wouldn't care what the reason was. She'd just be happy that Carmie wasn't moving. Her slightly dumpy best friend was going nowhere. Carmie listened and all she could hear was the sound of Fluff Bucket in the kitchen pushing the Chicken and Fish Buffet can across the counter. Then she felt a burst of confidence. Why couldn't her mom and Moondoggie still get together? She wasn't the worst liar, because things weren't that far off track. It wasn't the most impossible thing in the world to imagine that Carmie could live at the beach and have a boyfriend who liked her. This could happen. Carmie looked at the clock. It was almost nine, and her mother had been sleeping since she'd hung up the phone with Aunt Raleigh. Carmie had seen her sleep a thousand times. But what if tonight something was wrong? What if she'd gotten too tired? What had Aunt Raleigh said to her?

Carmie got out of bed and started down the hall to her mother's room. The door was closed, so Carmie knocked softly. The light on the nightstand was still on, and there were open bottles of vitamins everywhere. Carmie's mom was sleeping in her T-shirt. A strand of sun-streaked hair crossed her face. Her face looked old again, and as if she was in pain. Carmie felt frightened, but she told herself to hang loose. Her mother would be fine when she woke up, and they'd be back at the beach the next day.

*   *   *

"Carmie!" Elaine called the next morning. She knocked on Carmie's door. "Let's go, my dear. You've got ten minutes to get to orchestra." Carmie thought her mother's voice sounded strong again.

"Coming!" Carmie adjusted the top of her bikini in the mirror, then reached into her closet and put on clean jeans and a T-shirt. She took her viola case out and opened it, checking each string to make sure it wasn't out of tune.

"I'll be waiting for you in the car," Elaine called.

"Do you already have my board?" Carmie called back as her mother left the house. Carmie straightened her hair with her hand, and she felt happy as she opened the refrigerator door and took two Extreme Power Treats.

"You're going to like Princess Blue," she said to Fluff Bucket while she popped open the treat wrappers. Then she ran to the car.

She got a good look at her mom behind the wheel.

"First stop, rippin' rehearsal." Carmie laughed.

"Did you practice at all last night?" Elaine asked.

"A little," Carmie said.

"A little is not enough. Do you want to let your orchestra members down?"

"I'm ready for the recital," Carmie said shyly. "I told Daddy this wasn't any big deal and that he didn't have to come here."

"I'm not so concerned about your performing well for your father."

"I'm not going to let anybody down," Carmie said.

"Did you work on your movie story last night too?" Elaine asked.

"Not really," Carmie said. "I watched *Spider-Man* on cable again but then I didn't know how to start my screenplay."

"How about 'once upon a time'?" Elaine smiled.

"Mommy, I told you." Carmie tried to sound as if she thought her mother was funny. "Movies don't start with 'once upon a time.' They start with 'fade in.' "

Elaine pulled onto Haynes Street, where the school was at the end of the block. She put her foot on and then took it off the brake pedal.

"You'll pick me up at eleven, right?" Carmie asked.

"That's right," Elaine said. "If you want me to and it's too hot to walk."

Carmie turned and looked in the station wagon. The Jacobs wasn't in it.

"Where's the board?" Carmie froze. "I thought you got it."

"Not today," Elaine said. "I can pick you up and bring you home today."

"But why?" Carmie asked. "Why are we going home? Don't you feel good?"

"I do feel tired," Elaine said. "That's true. We don't have to go out there every day. Besides, I promised Aunt Raleigh I wouldn't go today. I'm going to go with her to the closing Tofu Tea."

"But why can't you go there tomorrow?"

"Because today is the closing tea. It will be closed tomorrow. Maybe we can go back to Malibu tomorrow or the next day."

"But tomorrow the big swell will be gone. Do you know what that means, dude?" Carmie felt as if she was going to cry.

Elaine stretched her hand out to Carmie and touched her shoulder gently.

"I know you like learning how to surf. And I'm happy about that. But it's a lot of driving every day. Just the gas alone . . ."

"But I have money for gas," Carmie said. "I have two hundred dollars in my savings. It's right there in my closet. I can pay for all the gas."

"It's not just the gas," Elaine said. "And you know that's not what your savings is for. Come on, Carmie. Be fair."

"I am." Carmie tried not to whine. She felt ridiculous, but she couldn't hold herself back. "Why don't you

215

understand? Don't you want to stay healthy? I know you can just get better and better."

"Sweetie, I feel perfectly fine, thank you, and even pro surfers have to take five."

"No, they hang ten!" Carmie said. She could feel her voice getting angrier. She looked at her mother and tried to catch her breath. "But don't you love the beach?" she asked softly.

"Of course I love the beach," Elaine said, pulling into the school driveway. "What is there not to love about the ocean?"

"Exactly," Carmie said. "Well then, you don't want to let anybody there down, do you?"

"Like who?" Elaine said. "You mean Moondoggie? I just saw him yesterday. Thanks to you, he made me a delicious peanut butter and jelly sandwich."

"But that's not even his specialty," Carmie said, and smiled. "He was going to make us a surprise abalone dinner today. Don't you love abalone? What *is* abalone?" Carmie tried not to laugh.

"It's a shellfish." Elaine smiled, as if she was remembering. "The guys dive for abalone in the water by the cliffs. Then they pound it out of the shell and fry it."

"Well, isn't that so much cooler than what we ever have for dinner?" Carmie begged. "Why do we have to eat like normal people? I've never pounded out a piece of fish in my life."

Elaine turned off the engine and rubbed her eyes. "That's enough, Carmie. Maybe we can go to Malibu tomorrow or the next day. Have a good rehearsal, sweetie. You have a gift here." She tapped the viola case. "Listen to Mr. Adler. Do you still want me to pick you up?"

"I don't know." Carmie fought back her tears. "No. Are you okay, Mommy?"

"I'll be fine," Elaine said. "If you don't need me to pick you up, maybe I'll just go with Aunt Raleigh earlier and we can get home earlier. Make yourself a sandwich. There's some delicious spelt bread. Maybe you'd like to call one of your other friends. And don't worry," she said softly. "Believe me. The ocean isn't going anywhere. Coady and Moondoggie aren't going anywhere."

"But I am," Carmie thought as she got out of the car. She made sure she didn't slam the door. "I've come too far to let this all go now."

Chapter 30

"No, violas!" Mr. Adler tapped his baton on the stand. Everybody stopped. "There's a rest between those two notes. See?" He pretended to look at the music. Carmie knew he was looking right at her, because there was only one other violist in the orchestra. Carmie looked at her music stand. Then she lifted her bow.

She imagined herself putting out her thumb for a ride. Somebody nice would have to pick her up and take her to Malibu. She cringed. She had seen that in the movies. But in the movies nobody ever had a surfboard that needed a ride too. What street could she even stand on?

"Okay, now, and now the music builds here," Mr. Adler said, lifting his arms higher and higher. He swung them from side to side. He closed his eyes as if he was off in some incredible heaven. Everybody tried not to giggle. Carmie saw Coady in the ocean at that moment. His eyes were wide open, staring at last into the crystal face of the perfect wave. What if this was the day?

Who else could give Carmie a ride? Aunt Raleigh was out. What about Uncle Roy? Even if he wasn't working, which he always was, he would just tell anyway. What about Laurie or Stephanie? She thought of her other friends, but they were all friends with Jenny, too. What if later they told her the truth? What was the truth?

*   *   *

"Hey, Fluffy B.," Carmie said as she unlocked the back door. Fluff Bucket jumped onto the counter, and Carmie opened a can of Fish Buffet. "Don't worry. I'll still get us out of here."

She went into the garage. The Jacobs was standing against the washing machine. Carmie could stand in front of the board on the road and then nobody would see it until she had already gotten into the car. She would only take a ride from a girl or a woman. Carmie lifted the board. She closed the garage door. Her heart started to pound. But what would she tell her mother if she ever found out? Her mother would kill her if somebody didn't stab her to death in the car first. Carmie knew better. She promised herself she would not get into a car with anybody even slightly weird looking, even if she was a woman. Then she ran to the computer. *Bus Schedules*, she typed on the Internet. *Van Nuys to Malibu*. There was no bus to Malibu. She could take four transfers for different buses that would get her as far as Santa Monica. But it would take three hours to get there. But then if she just hitchhiked from there down the Pacific Coast Highway, it wouldn't be so dangerous. But what if surfboards had to ride the bus outside in front with the bicycles? What if the Jacobs fell off?

Carmie listened to the silence of the house. She tried to think. Her brain wanted to rest, but she couldn't stop now.

Her cell phone rang.

"Hello?" Carmie answered.

"Can you hear me now?" a voice called, muffled.

"Hey!" Carmie almost squealed. "Jenny! Where are you?"

"We're in the mountains. We're on our way home."

"How come so early?" Carmie panicked.

"Because!" Jenny laughed. "Both of my cousins got totally sick. So gross." Then her voice got quiet. "Plus I miss you. Are you in Malibu already?"

"I'm on my way down there right now," Carmie said quickly.

"Wow." Jenny sounded as if reality was really settling in. "You're with your mom?"

"Not exactly," Carmie said, trying to sound completely together.

"Well then, if your mom's not driving you, who is?"

"I can't quite say." Carmie's voice quivered.

"Whoa!" Jenny said loudly. "I get it. Oh my God. You're with that guy Coady. He drove all the way out to get you, right?"

"Not a hundred percent exactly." Carmie pretended she had to talk quietly. She knew this was her chance to tell the truth, but she didn't know how to say it.

"So then, it's Maxwell at the wheel?" Jenny said. "Maxwell drove you halfway!"

"Of course." Carmie laughed. "Maxwell drove me to B.H. Then I gave him the rest of the afternoon off."

"Well, whatever's going on over there," Jenny said, laughing, "you're the best because you're the bomb!" Then her voice started to break up.

"Jenny?" Carmie listened. "Jenny?" Carmie missed her friend. "Jenny, I am the bomb and you are the genius," she said, and hung up the phone. Maxwell. Maxwell was the answer.

Carmie looked online for the numbers for limousine services, then dialed the first one on her cell.

"Do you want us to come get you in a town car?" the voice answered. "That will be roughly sixty dollars."

"Can my surfboard fit too?" Carmie asked.

"You mean just to put in there lengthwise?" the woman asked as if that was insane. "You a real Malibu surfer?"

"Uh-huh," Carmie answered.

"Oh, no, then, honey." The woman sounded impressed. "The town car isn't long enough. Besides, you'll be a lot more comfy in the stretch."

*　*　*

Carmie waited in front of the house with the Jacobs. She had on her dressiest white blouse and best blue jeans. She patted her back pocket to make sure her cell phone was sticking out just the right amount.

The street was quiet. Carmie hoped it would stay that way. The car had to come before any of the neighbors came home and saw her leave. Carmie looked at her house. Fluff Bucket was sitting in the window, watching her.

A car turned onto Apricot. It was the longest, shiniest black car ever seen on that street. It was going too slowly, looking at all the numbers. It was the kind of car Carmie had seen only once before, on Jenny's street when they were taping *The B.H.*

"Whoa!" Carmie cried with a giggle. The car stopped and the driver got out. He was short and he wore a suit and a driver's hat.

"Hoffman?" He looked Carmie up and down. Then he looked at the board and opened the door for her. There was enough room in this car for the longest longboard Carmie had ever seen. There was enough room for a boat. Carmie lifted the Jacobs.

"Allow me, miss," the driver said. He placed the board carefully against a seat. There were seats on both sides of the car, facing each other, and mirrors on both sides so people could see themselves when they were riding. There was one long seat across the back for the passenger who was the most famous.

"Make yourself comfortable," the driver said, helping her into the famous seat. Inside, the first things Carmie saw were peanuts and glasses and bottles and Extreme Power Treat Bars.

There were a TV, and a radio playing soft music, and a full can of Diet Coke right by her side. It was sunny outside, but the windows inside were tinted so she could look out but nobody could see inside.

"You know the price, correct?" the driver asked.

"It's exactly one hundred, right?" Carmie patted her pocket.

"Yes, excluding gratuity," the driver said.

A chill ran down Carmie's back. She tried to remember what *gratuity* meant.

"I have enough money." Carmie's voice trembled.

"Cool," the driver said. Then he pulled off the street.

Carmie smiled. Everything looked different behind brown glass. Even smaller.

"Well, I guess I must be taking you back home," the driver said. "You're never going to see anybody say 'Surf's up in the Valley,' " he said, laughing at his own joke.

"You've got that right," Carmie said confidently.

"What's your number on the highway?" the driver asked.

"Huh?" Carmie froze.

"Your address," the driver said. "On the Pacific Coast Highway."

"Oh, you can just drop me off at Malibu Beach, please. I think I'll catch a wave first. Then I'm going to a party."

"Boy, I wish I could just wait for you," the driver said, laughing. "I'd love to go to a party at Malibu. You're so lucky. What's your name?"

"Carmie."

"Carmie?" he repeated. "Nice to meet you, Carmie. I'm Max. My real name's Maxwell but my friends call me Max."

"Hi, Max," Carmie said, stunned. She looked out the window. It was as if her whole body was smiling. What was the likelihood of this happening even in a movie? Spending all her savings couldn't be a mistake, because this was going to end up being the perfect day. Even if her mother ever found out, which she didn't have to, she would thank Carmie when she realized that Carmie was only putting into place the rest of her mother's life. Carmie sat back in the seat and looked at the Jacobs sitting there. This was the best ride it had ever had.

The traffic getting to the canyon was almost bumper to bumper. Carmie saw people from the other cars trying to look into the brown glass and see who she was. This was just like in one of her famous movie scripts.

"They can't see me in here, right, Max?" Carmie called to the front of the car.

She looked at her board. She thought of her mother and Aunt Raleigh. She wished Jenny was there to laugh with her. What was she even going to tell Jenny when Jenny came home the next day? For a second Carmie felt lonely and afraid, but she quickly reminded herself she couldn't worry about that that day.

* * *

When they turned right onto the Pacific Coast Highway, Carmie's heart raced with excitement. It was ten minutes after three, the latest she had ever been at Malibu. Everything looked different. The waves were big, but not as ferocious as the day before. The traffic was heavy, but Carmie didn't have to worry about keeping her eye out for a parking space, so it didn't matter. A superlong white limo drove beside them on the right. Carmie couldn't see well into the window, but she was sure the person in there had seen her and they had nodded to each other as if they had a secret code. Carmie opened the lit mirror and checked her blouse. She smoothed her hair with her hand.

"Malibu Beach," Max said, turning left into the parking

lot. "You're home!" He opened the window. "Look at all these people!"

The girls, in their perfect bikinis, and their surf guys walking down the middle of the parking lot stopped to let the limo through, all trying to look into the windows.

"Right here is fine," Carmie said, pointing to the entrance by the food trucks. She reached into her back pocket and counted out the hundred dollars. Her fingers were shaking.

"How much is the gratuity, Max?" Carmie asked in her most sophisticated voice. "That's the tip, right?"

"That's right," Max said. "It's usually fifteen percent, miss. That would be a hundred and fifteen dollars."

Carmie handed him $115. Now Coady or somebody would definitely have to give her a ride home. She couldn't worry about it now.

Max opened the back door and Carmie pretended to look past the faces. Max reached for her hand and helped her out of the car. He stepped inside and lifted out the board.

"Surf's up." He smiled, handing her the board. "It's been my pleasure being your driver today. And you have my number should you ever wish to return."

"Thank you, Max." Carmie smiled.

She started toward the beach. It felt cool to be there without her mother.

"Now I've seen it all." A girl laughed behind her. "Who is that? Somebody?"

"Could be," a guy said. "Or else it's just a kook with a lot of dinero."

225

Chapter 31

✱
✱ ✱ ✱
✱ ✱

"That's a party wave, bruddah," two surfer guys called, running past Carmie with their boards.

Carmie pretended to be totally okay with stopping to look at the waves. Everybody seemed to be with somebody. Could that really be where the big party was? Was she too late? It was only three fifteen. A hundred surfers tried to take off in the lineup. Carmie looked for Coady's glasses. Two surfer girls sailed on the outsides of the wave, leaving everybody else behind.

"All right, women!" Carmie cheered softly. "Yes!" She tried to see if they were Jill and Robin. Once, long ago, that could have been her mother and Aunt Raleigh. Could her mother ever have been that stoked? Carmie opened her towel. She sat down and took the movie notebook out of her backpack.

FAMOUS MOVIE SCRIPT
MALIBU BEACH PARTY
By Malibu Carmie Hoffman

Outside. Malibu Beach. The party is about to start. CARMIE HOFFMAN, dressed in perfect . . . Once upon a time . . .

Carmie stopped writing and stood up. She carried her board to the water. Just then she recognized someone coming out of the water. He shook his blond-white hair and hoisted his board under his arm.

"Hi, Jon," Carmie said.

"Hey." He looked at Carmie as if he was trying to figure out who she was.

"I met you first on *The B.H.*," Carmie said.

"Oh, yeah, right!" he said as if remembering was good news. "Your mother swiped my board. Where's your buddy?"

"You mean Jenny?" Carmie asked. "She's still on vacation."

"Yeah, right," he said. "She's still in New Mexico?"

"Colorado. She's actually on her way back home."

"Oh yeah?" Jon smiled. Then he turned to look at someone coming up the beach. It was Barb. She was walking right toward them in her pink-and-lime-striped bikini. She was carrying a cardboard tray with food from the food truck.

"Hey, Jonny." She gave him a big smile so he could see how bright her teeth were. "I got you your Coke and fries." She handed them to him from the box. Then she pulled out a hot dog for herself and took a dainty bite.

227

"Hey, give me that," Jon said, laughing. He swiped it from her hand. "I've been surfing out there. I'm a growing boy. I've got to mack."

"But that's mine," she said, trying to sound sexy and whiny at the same time. "I'm hungry too, you know."

"I'm doing this for your own good," Jon said, shoving the rest of the dog into his mouth. "You've got a hot body. You don't want to get fat, do you?"

Carmie cringed. She could not wait to get away from Jon. How could anyone so gorgeous be so ugly?

"Yo," Jon called. "If your friend comes back by tonight, you guys should come to the party. Tell her it's at my house."

"Jooooon," Barb whined, giving Carmie a long dirty look.

"Okay," Carmie said, then turned and headed back to her towel. She lifted the Jacobs and her backpack and started the long walk to the legends' blanket. *Somebody* would have to be down there.

"Yo!" a voice called. "Yo, Carmie!"

Carmie turned and saw Coady. She felt relieved. He was jogging toward her with his surfboard under his arm. He had on his red and black striped baggies, and beads of water glistened on his chest. His black glasses cord bounced back and forth against his strong neck.

"Hey!" Carmie couldn't help smiling. She felt as if she was in a dream.

"I thought that was you," Coady said, and smiled.

"How were the waves?" Carmie asked.

"Pretty kickin'," Coady said. "But not worth fighting for with all those kooks in the water. It's a barnyard sausage-fest out there."

"I hear that," Carmie said, and laughed. "That must make it pretty frustrating when you've got the commitment and all you live for is to catch the perfect wave."

"You get used to it." Coady smiled. "But I cashed in at the zoo. Are you going up by the pier? The surf's not as big, but there's hardly anybody up there except Moondoggie and all those guys."

"That's where I was going." Carmie smiled.

"All right," Coady said. He was close enough now to see how especially pretty she looked. He could kiss her if he wanted, Carmie thought.

"You going to take that Jacobs out today? I can teach you a couple more things. You want to learn?"

"If you don't mind," Carmie said in her most polite tone of voice. "Do you think it's calm enough out there for me not to get mutilated or anything?"

"You should be okay," Coady said, laughing. "I won't let you do anything crazy. You won't get cactus-juiced or anything."

"Cool," Carmie said. "What's that?"

"It's like getting rag-dolled," Coady said gently. "You get too Mack-trucked to surf."

"Oh," Carmie said.

"There's guys back there getting hammered," Coady said. "But that's because they're groms on breaks that are too big for them. Where we go will be much flatter, as always. You'll see. Besides, you have nothing to worry about. You have good surf karma."

"Thanks," Carmie said, as if she knew exactly what *surf karma* meant.

229

The legends' blanket was spread out, but nobody was on it except Too Loose.

"Hey, dude, check it out." Too Loose nodded at his guitar strings. "Dick Dale, man. Classic riff."

"Awesome." Coady smiled.

"Where's Moondoggie?" Carmie asked.

"Don't know." Coady shrugged as if it had never even crossed his mind that an adult was missing. "I think he was on dawn patrol this morning. He's probably just up at the house sleeping or something. You going to leave your duds?"

"Sure." Carmie unzipped her jeans. She took them off as quickly as she could while Coady looked at the water. She patted her jean pockets for her cell phone. She felt the money. Then she looked over at Too Loose.

"Are you still going to be here?" she asked.

"No problemo," Too Loose said, nodding toward the blanket. "You're safe here."

Coady lifted the Jacobs onto his head and carried it to the water.

"See? I told you it was much calmer here," Coady called. Hardly anyone was out. The top of the ocean looked like glass. The sun beat down harder than it had on any day Carmie had been there; ordinarily they'd be home by now. She imagined her mother coming in the door, looking tired. Then she would start trying to find Carmie. Carmie remembered herself promising Aunt Raleigh that she would not run off to the beach, in exchange for borrowing her

Jacobs. She shook off those thoughts and walked farther out. Coady ran a little way ahead. Only the ends of his hair were wet. Did he even wonder where her mother was? Carmie told herself not to worry. By the time the party came, Coady would kiss her, and more than once.

Coady dropped the board, then patted it for Carmie to hop on.

"Is this your day?" Coady smiled.

"I hope so," Carmie said. Then she swallowed hard. It had to be her day. If her mother found out where she was, the next day might be too late.

"You going to put your leash on?" Coady asked.

"I don't know," Carmie said. "What do you think?"

"It's probably better," Coady said. Then he turned to look. "Come on," he said, sounding excited. "Don't worry. This could be perfect. Hold on to the rails."

Carmie grabbed the sides of the board tightly.

"Feel it?" Coady steadied the tail. "Feel it?"

"Yeah!" Carmie said. The ocean was gently rumbling up behind her.

"Okay . . . paddle!" Coady called. "Paddle! Paddle! Paddle!"

Carmie paddled as hard as she could.

"Okay, now!" Coady called. "Good girl. Now!"

Carmie felt herself leap off her stomach. Then she was on her haunches like a wobbly frog.

"Stand!" Coady yelled after her. "Stand!"

Carmie stood halfway; then she fell backward off the board. It leaped in front of her and headed toward shore. Carmie held her breath. She was in the other world now,

231

just waiting for the ocean to give her back to the sun. She bobbed up. She spit water and smoothed her hair with her hand.

"Almost!" Coady called back to her. He chased the board.

"Yeah. Almost 'da bomb.' " Carmie laughed.

"I can't believe this." Coady paddled to her.

"You can't believe me?" Carmie tried to laugh. "I'm not a very good swimmer. You mean I'm the worst girl you've ever tried to teach?"

"No." Coady's voice got serious. "You're the funniest. And you're the only girl I've ever tried to teach."

"Really?" Carmie felt the sides of her mouth wanting to smile too hard.

"There's something about you," he said, getting up close. "I don't know. You're different."

Carmie felt her arms tingling.

"I can't believe it," Coady said again. "You had this board just sitting in a garage all these years in the Valley." He looked at the board; then he looked at Carmie as if he was trying to put everything together. "When the whole time it belonged out here with you. How do you live in the Val?"

"Well, it's not easy," Carmie said, trying to joke. Her heart beat fast. "It's not like living out here or anything."

"I mean, but what do people do out there?" Coady asked.

"Not too much." Carmie laughed. "You know. The regular torture. Go to school, go to orchestra, hang out at the mall in Sherman Oaks. Have you ever seen it?"

"Sherman Oaks?" Coady asked. "Where's that?"

"In the Valley," Carmie said as if she knew he had to be joking.

"I've never been to the Valley," Coady said.

"Oh."

Carmie jumped onto the board on her stomach. She rolled into the water.

"Let me try that again," she said, hitting the board. "Don't you go anywhere without me." She pretended to laugh. She coughed and spit water from her mouth. She felt the sun pounding down on her. She had to stand up on the next wave. She just had to.

"The party later should be cool," Carmie said quickly. "I'm glad my mother didn't come today. That would have been a drag. Even though I think she really likes your dad. Do you think your dad is bummed she's not here today?"

"What do you mean?" Coady asked, his voice getting serious.

"Oh, sorry," Carmie said. She felt confused and frightened. "I meant Moondoggie. Not your dad."

Coady got up close to her. "Moondoggie?" he asked. "Sean? He's not my father."

Carmie froze.

"You thought he was my dad?" Coady asked with a chuckle. "No, dude. I haven't seen my old man for years."

"Why not?" Carmie asked.

"The guy's a total burnout. He just took off. My mom ran off with some other loser. She sort of comes back and forth. So Moondoggie just watches out for me. He's cool. But he's not my father. He's just my uncle, dude. Didn't your mom tell you?"

"I don't think that she even knew," Carmie said. "I guess I never asked her."

Coady looked out at the water. "All right! Feel that wave?" He put his hand on the tail of Carmie's board.

"Is it going to be too big?" Carmie asked.

"It's going to be bigger than the last one. It could get hairy out here with no board."

"Coady," Carmie said. "I don't think I—"

"Okay, wait!" Coady watched the horizon. "The wave's starting to build. You're going to be fine. Wait till it's curling over you. Ready? Ready? Paddle!" Coady shouted. "Paddle hard, Carmie! Paddle your heart out!"

"Okay," Carmie called. She felt her arms crying out for help. "Now what do I do, Coady?"

A gigantic wave started to curl over Carmie's board like a tunnel. It was louder than anything. She couldn't hear Coady anymore.

"Stand!" she heard herself say. "Stand up!"

Carmie held the rails. She leaped off her stomach. Then she stood up fast. She leaned forward into the wave. She put her arms out as if they were wings. She felt as if she was in a dream. A dream in which life was not at all what it seemed.

"Yeeeeehiiiiiiiiiii!"

Then she was knocked off the wave and into the water. She held her breath. The underworld thrashed her around as if it was a washing machine that could never stop. How could something that so thrilled her turn on her so quickly?

Then Carmie heard the muffled sound of her head hitting what had to be a rock. Her body spun away and then back. The pointy rock stabbed her head again. Then everything went dark.

*　*　*

"You okay?" Coady called. Carmie bobbed in and out of the water. She gasped for air. He was swimming toward her; his glasses were off his face and bouncing on his chest.

"Am I bleeding?" She looked at her fingers. They were red from squeezing the board so tightly. She touched her head. She felt as if she was spinning. Then, suddenly, her feet found the ocean floor. She jumped up and down in the water.

"Let me see." Coady got right up next to her. "Stand still." He lifted her hair gently off her forehead. He studied her forehead as if it was something he had just found in the ocean that was so precious it couldn't just belong to a body.

"You got a little thrashing," he said, trying to laugh. "But, hey! You stood up! You rocked! Look at me! At least you had the board! I had to bodysurf it. Do I look all rag-dolled?"

"No," Carmie said. She touched his arm. "You okay?"

"You dizzy?" Coady put his arm around Carmie's waist. "Come on. We've got to get you in."

"Okay," Carmie said. She hoped Coady couldn't feel any fat on her sides. "The rocks tried to kill me!" she said.

"You didn't hit any rocks," Coady said. "You got punched by your board."

"Am I going to live?" Carmie joked to hide her shock. "Oh my God. Where's my board? If I broke that Jacobs, my aunt is going to kill me."

"You're going to live." Coady kissed Carmie's head. "And I doubt anyone is going to kill you. Your board's probably just on its way to shore."

"Good," Carmie said. This was like being in a movie. A movie in which she was melting and shivering at the same time.

When they got closer to the sand, the board was waiting for them. "Just sit right here and watch this thing," Coady said. "It's better if I go get help."

"Whatever you do, don't call my mother," Carmie begged.

"Why would I call your mother?" Coady asked as if that was the last thing on his mind. Then he ran up to the blanket. Carmie wished she hadn't said that about her mother and ruined the moment. She turned and saw Coady saying something to Candy and Too Loose. Then Coady ran toward the cliffs that led to the highway.

Chapter 32

*   ✷   ✷   ✷   ✷   ✷

"Emergency vehicle!" A voice came over a loudspeaker. Carmie awoke and saw a lifeguard jeep driving up the beach. "People, clear the way, please," the voice called. The light on top of the vehicle was flashing. Then the jeep turned on its siren. Carmie thought that if it was coming for her, she would just die.

People followed the jeep. Carmie looked to see if Coady was coming back for her. The jeep stopped a few feet away and the lifeguard jumped out. He lifted a kit from the back. He crouched down like a frog and looked at Carmie's forehead.

"I think you've made a mistake stopping at me," Carmie said.

"Are you okay?" he asked. "Can you tell me your full name?"

"Carmie Hoffman."

"Carmie," the lifeguard repeated. "Did you lose

consciousness?" He looked right into her eyes. Then he did a double take, as if he couldn't figure out how he knew her. It was the same lifeguard as before. He wrapped a blood pressure cuff around her arm. Then he pumped it.

"Okay there," he said, checking the gauge, then taking off the band. "Is your mom here?"

"No," Carmie said. "I got a ride."

"Well, if you tell me your number, we can call your mother for you."

"That's okay," Carmie said. "You don't have to call her."

"Why's that?" he asked.

"Because I'm okay. Seriously. But sometimes she's not that well and I don't want her to worry about me."

The lifeguard looked at Carmie. "Oh, right! It's you! You're the girl who was worried your mother was too sick to score the hot surf and then that she was kidnapped off her towel. Right?"

"Well, yes," Carmie said softly.

"I'm just glad you're okay," the lifeguard said, smiling. A group of people stood in a circle, watching Carmie as if she was in a zoo. "But we have to call your mother."

"Hey," a girl said to her boyfriend, loudly enough for the lifeguard to hear, "isn't that the chick who we saw get out of that limo? How lame is that that she constantly needs to be getting attention?"

The lifeguard looked at Carmie and shook his head. Carmie didn't look him in the eye.

"I think I have enough money to get home," Carmie told the lifeguard. "I just have to call the number on my cell. My mother is never home and she doesn't use a cell phone."

"Well, we'll still need to call an adult who knows you so they know the limo, or whatever, is on its way." The lifeguard tried not to smile. He opened a large Band-Aid and pressed it gently onto Carmie's head.

"I know adults here," Carmie insisted. Her heart was pounding.

She looked up and saw Coady and Moondoggie running toward the scene, and she took a deep breath. Moondoggie had probably come to drive her home.

"It's okay," Moondoggie said, running up to the lifeguard. "She's not hurt too bad, right? She just ate some sand. I'll watch out for her for now."

"Who is she?" two surfer girls whispered. "Is she somebody famous?"

"Cool." The lifeguard reached to shake Moondoggie's hand. "You're Sean Woodward, right?"

"Yeah, dude," Moondoggie said, smiling. "I know her mom."

Moondoggie lifted Carmie as if she was a pillow. He carried her to the legends' blanket. Everybody was just looking as if this was a great scene out of *Blue Crush* in which the nobody risked her life and was rescued by somebody and then turned out to be somebody herself.

"Here." Coady handed her a cup of water. "Drink this." She put the cup up to her lips and drank. He took the empty cup away.

"I'll go get your stick, Carmie," he said, heading for the shore. "No worries. It didn't eat it."

Carmie tried to call after him, but she was too tired to get the words out of her mouth.

"Catch a few z's, cutie," Moondoggie said. "You'll feel better. Everything is going to be all right, honey. You're covered. We've got you a ride."

Chapter 33

"Carmie?" Carmie felt a smooth cool finger touch her forehead.

She opened one eye. She heard the seagulls crying over the breaking surf.

"Sweetie, are you okay?" Elaine asked.

"Mommy?" Carmie sat up too quickly, startled. She suddenly felt dizzy and nauseated. "I almost got killed."

"I suppose you could have," Elaine said gently, smoothing Carmie's hair with her hand. "We are very lucky. I told you those waves can be dangerous if you don't know what you're doing out there. And sometimes even if you do know what you're doing out there."

"Yeah, but what are you doing here?" Carmie asked.

"That's a question I was just about to ask you," Elaine said. "Moondoggie called me. The last time I saw you, I thought you were just going to play your viola."

Carmie tried to lift her head and look around her. The lifeguard jeep was gone. Moondoggie was at the other side of the legends' blanket, listening to Too Loose play songs by Dick Dale, King of the Surf Guitar.

"I did go to rehearsal but then I just had to come back here," Carmie said, lifting herself onto her elbows. "Don't you understand, Mommy?" She used all her strength to plead to her mother finally to hear her. "We belong here."

"What are you talking about?" Elaine asked with a nervous laugh.

"This is where I should have been born," Carmie said. "This is where we should have lived all along. If you would have just married Moondoggie, Daddy would never have left."

"Is that what you think?" Elaine's body tensed. "Is that what this is all about?" She reached for Carmie's hand. "I'm afraid life is sometimes not that easy, sweetie."

"But why not?" Carmie held back her tears. "Everybody's life is easy here."

"That may be how it looks to you from the outside. But believe me," Elaine said more loudly, as if she didn't care who heard her, "on the inside Coady's and Moondoggie's lives are not all easy. Nobody's life is completely perfect."

"But yours could have been if you made a commitment."

"Your father and I made a commitment," Elaine said.

"But it didn't stick," Carmie argued.

"It may not have stuck forever but it was wonderful for what it was," Elaine said. "Neither one of us would ever change what we got out of our marriage. Not now or ever. We wanted you and we love you. And we always will. I loved your father very much. We didn't know from the beginning that we weren't committed enough to the same important ideals."

"But if you'd married Moondoggie," Carmie said, "you could have both been surfers. Then you would have had the same ideals."

Elaine looked at Moondoggie. He nodded and sang to the guitar riffs. He looked handsome.

"Because two people like to do the same thing doesn't necessarily mean they share the same ideals. I don't know if I would have liked surfing every day for the rest of my life. And besides, I couldn't marry Moondoggie," Elaine said.

"How come?" Carmie asked. "Didn't he ever ask you?"

"He didn't need to," Elaine said. "He knew I would have said no."

"But why?" Carmie asked in disbelief.

"Because, sweetie. Moondoggie never wanted to have a child. And if I hadn't had you"—Elaine swallowed hard— "I would have missed the greatest gift of my life."

Three perfect tears rolled down Elaine's face. Carmie looked deep into her eyes. It was as if she was looking underneath the ocean. Her mom looked beautiful.

"I'm sorry, Mommy," Carmie said, and began to cry. She held her head in case anybody looked and thought she was just crying for no reason.

"Hey!" Moondoggie called, coming over. "You're going to be just fine," he said, and patted Carmie's head. "You've got good surf karma."

"I guess," Carmie said, afraid Moondoggie would see she was crying. If he hadn't wanted a baby before, he wouldn't want to be around a big baby now.

"You'll see," Moondoggie said, smiling at Elaine. "She's going to turn into a good little surfer."

"If that's what she wants," Elaine said, smiling back at him. "But I think no more today. Ready?" Elaine asked Carmie. "Come on. I think it's time to go."

"You want me to carry Carmie up to the car?" Moondoggie asked.

"That's okay," Carmie said in her most together tone of voice. The last thing she wanted now was for everybody on the beach to notice her.

"Well, how about your board? Want me to carry that?" Moondoggie smiled.

Elaine laughed. She hoisted the board under her arm. "Brings back good memories," she said. "Helps me stay in shape."

"Good." Moondoggie smiled at her as if they knew a secret code.

Carmie looked around for Coady, trying not to be obvious.

"He went back down to the circus," Moondoggie said, looking at the ocean. "A whole bunch of egg beaters out there who'll never get up on a single wave," he said, shaking his head. "You sure you don't want to wait for him?"

"We'll probably come back," Carmie said, looking at her mother for her reaction.

"What do you mean, 'probably'?" Moondoggie laughed as if he was nervous. "You've got to come back. Today was sort of a bust, but that's what every good surfer goes through, right, Elaine? It's like an initiation. Today you passed the test. You're one of us now. You're our Malibu

Carmie," he said, as if he was dubbing her royalty. "Hey, dudes," he called to everybody on the blanket. "Dig it. This is Malibu Carmie."

"Righteous." Cotton Candy, Aloha and Too Loose all cheered.

"That's cool." Carmie tried not to show how excited she was. Moondoggie started up the beach with her and Elaine.

"Coady will be glad to know you're okay," Moondoggie said. "So when can I tell him you're coming back, Malibu?"

"It's hard to say," Elaine answered. "Carmie needs to rest up, and besides, she has a performance to get ready for."

"Mom . . . ," Carmie said, trying to save herself from embarrassment.

"I bet you didn't know," Elaine said proudly. "Malibu Carmie is also a gifted musician. The Valley Orchestra has got a concert coming up."

"Far out," Moondoggie said.

"I still have two more tickets if Jenny and her mom can't go," Carmie said to Elaine. "Can I invite Moondoggie?"

"Thanks, cutie," Moondoggie answered. "That's very nice of you, but why don't you guys come here? Coady and I will make you that abalone dinner I promised. Besides," he chuckled. "I don't do so well more than a few miles east of the Pacific Coast Highway. Makes me break out in hives."

*   *   *

Carmie and Elaine walked slowly up the beach in silence. Carmie looked at the ocean to see if she could spot Coady.

245

She kept thinking she saw him, but then she couldn't be sure. Her heart pounded. Whatever he was saying, he was too far away for her to hear his voice clearly.

"I'm sorry you had to drive all the way here," Carmie finally said.

"It was worth it." Elaine smiled. "I hope it was for you, too, since you probably just gave away half your savings. When Moondoggie called, he said he'd heard you had come here in a limo!"

"I'm sorry, Mommy," Carmie whimpered. Now her head was hurting again. "I still have about a hundred dollars." She tried not to cry.

"That's good." Elaine laughed. "We may just need it for the limo going back."

"The limo?" Carmie stopped walking.

"Yeah." Elaine reached for Carmie's hand. "Aunt Raleigh's limo. She drove me. She's waiting. There was no place to park. She deserves a nice tip."

"Cool." Carmie sighed. "The Jacobs doesn't have a ding in it."

"You got everything?" Elaine double-checked. "Your movie notebook is in your backpack?"

"Uh-huh," Carmie said, feeling relaxed for the first time all day. "I got a new start today. I started it 'once upon a time.'"

"Once upon a time?" Elaine questioned. "Once upon a time what?"

"Once upon a time there was a surfer woman and she had a daughter."

Chapter 34

✶
✶ ✶ ✶
✶ ✶

"Fluff Bucket's house," Carmie answered her cell. "Fluff speaking."

"Meeoow!" Jenny laughed too loudly. "Malibu Fluff Bucket. Dude. What are you still doing here in the Val?"

"Am I never going to hear the end of that one for my whole life?" Carmie asked.

"Maybe you will." Jenny laughed. "As soon as I forgive you for being a bad little liar even though I thought you might be making the whole thing up to begin with. Besides, I know you can't survive high school without me. So you'll have to wait until you and Coady can get married. It's not going to hurt to probably be the only freshman in the history of Van Nuys High with a guy at the beach."

"Righto." Carmie laughed. "I think he's okay just as a boyfriend. Plus my dad's coming in tomorrow and my mom isn't even getting sick." Carmie laughed again with joy. "I think it's because of Moondoggie."

"So listen to this," Jenny said. "They're driving all the

movie trucks onto my street. They're taping *The B.H.* again in a half hour. Is this so great? So get over here. Fast!" She sounded too excited to think about anything else.

"I can't," Carmie said. She lifted her viola from the closet, wiping the dust off the case. "I have dress rehearsal."

"What do you do in dress rehearsal?" Jenny asked. "Do you all get dressed?"

"Exactly." Carmie laughed.

"That sounds like fun," Jenny said. "Can I come? I've never been to one of those things before."

"Sure!" Carmie said. "But are you sure you want to miss *The B.H.* for that? I mean, then you're going to see the real concert in two days."

"I'm with you." Jenny laughed. "Meet me on the corner."

"Righteous," Carmie said. "Just give me five minutes."

"Bye, Mom!" Carmie ran into the kitchen and grabbed two Extreme Power Treats. Then she opened her notebook.

THE BU
Famous Television Show By Malibu Carmie Hoffman

LAST SCENE:

Outside. Malibu Beach. Star of the show, beautiful CARMIE HOFFMAN, walks down the beach with her brand-new board under her arm. In the distance, on the legends' blanket, we see JENNY and Jenny's new boyfriend, FRED. CARMIE'S MOM and MOONDOGGIE are waving. Everybody's there, including some new friends who took the bus from Van Nuys High. The Bu theme song, totally cool surf guitar music, begins. Suddenly COADY ap-

pears on the beach with his board. He smiles at Carmie, then starts to walk with her to the shore.

COADY

You stoked? You ready?

CARMIE

Totally. (She smooths her perfect hair with her hand.) Let's go for it!

Carmie closed her notebook. Then she picked up her viola, left the house and ran as fast as she could to the corner.

About the Author

Leah Komaiko is the author of many books for children of all ages and for adults, including the Annie Bananie books and *Earl's Too Cool for Me*. Many years ago, Leah had a wet suit and a surfboard and a house on the beach. Now she lives above sea level in the Valley in Los Angeles. Righteous!